HOMEWRECKERS

ARON BEAUREGARD

BAD DREAM BOOKS

For Shane McKenzie.

"Sometimes you will never know the value of a moment until it becomes a memory."

— Dr. Seuss

MOVING IN

Bruce Huxley set the last box down on the table and winced. Placing his fist against his back, he turned to his wife.

"Shit, tell me you brought the Icy Hot," Bruce said.

Liv sat at the table, a wide grin on her face as she played cards with their son, Dustin.

"What's Icy Hot?" Dustin asked.

Bruce approached the table. "Something you hopefully won't need for at least another thirty years."

"Thirty years?! That's old . . ." Dustin said.

Liv looked at Dustin like she was offended by the statement. "Excuse me," she scoffed, sticking her tongue out at him. "Must be so nice to be four years old."

"Four and a half," Dustin corrected.

"Either way, you've got time," Bruce said. "I don't." He switched his focus from his son to his wife. "So . . . is that a yes or a no?"

Footsteps crept up from behind him, and a hand reached around holding a tube of Icy Hot. Liv's mother, Alice, smiled as she maneuvered her big frame and worked her way to the table.

"Awesome." Bruce instantly applied some. "Thanks, Alice."

"I want some!" Dustin said.

"It's medicine, not candy, honey," Liv said. "You're only supposed to use it if you need it."

"It's the least I can do after making you help me move—and during winter of all times," Alice said. "I'm not sure how I would've pulled this off without you."

"That's what family's for," Liv said. "You got back here awful fast."

Alice grinned, taking a seat at the table. "Antonio's isn't too far away. You must be starving after all that work."

Liv stayed quiet, looking down at her cards.

Turning to Bruce, Alice pointed at the boxes of pizza on the stove in the kitchen. "What about you?"

"I could eat," Bruce said.

"Yeah, me too!" Dustin added.

Bruce knew Liv was trying to watch what she ate. Ever since Dustin was born, her body had undergone some dramatic changes. It had been a bit of a struggle for her to keep the weight off—something she'd never struggled with before. Despite his reassurances that she would always be beautiful to him, Liv seemed depressed about it at times. Still, Bruce was too tired and hungry to skip out on the food.

"And—and after we eat, we watch a movie!" Dustin said, clapping his hands.

Bruce could feel his back starting to tighten. Even the thought of sitting on a couch made him grimace. "Buddy, we might need to have an early night tonight. Your mother and I have a lot of stuff to help Grandma unpack tomorrow, and we're gonna need our rest."

"Pleeeeeeeeaaase," Dustin begged.

"Maybe tomorrow night," Liv said.

Dustin pouted, heartbroken.

"I've got an idea," Alice said. "How about we let Mom and Dad hit the hay after we eat, and I'll stay up and watch a movie with you?"

"Yay!" Dustin yelled.

"Mom, are you sure?" Liv asked. "It's okay if you're tired too. Really."

"All I did was a lot of watching," Alice said. "I'll be fine." She turned to her grandson. "What do you say, Dustin? Should we go . . . back to the future?"

"Yaaaaaaay!" Dustin cheered, then turned his attention to the TV playing in the background. "What's that?"

On the screen was a commercial advertising the upcoming Stanley Cup Finals.

"That's hockey, buddy," Bruce said. "It's a sport that people play."

"Looks like fun," Dustin said.

"It's pretty good, but I was always partial to wrestling." Bruce flexed his arm and pumped it.

Liv rolled her eyes.

"What? I was a college phenom," Bruce said.

Liv giggled. "Sure you were."

"Hey, at least my college interests weren't just smoking cigarettes and trying to look cool."

Alice glared at Liv, taken aback. "You were a smoker?!"

"Thanks, Bruce," Liv said, turning her attention back to her mother. "It was the only way I could relax when all those accounting tests were stressing me out. Bruce almost didn't want to date me because of it. Boy, that would've been the biggest mistake he ever—"

"Anyway . . ." Bruce interjected, looking at Dustin. "Even though it's not wrestling, they do scrap occasionally. Maybe when you're a little older, you can give hockey a try."

After rubbing the top of Dustin's head, Bruce set a couple slices of pizza on a paper plate. As he ate, he took a minute to admire his family. Despite his aching back, he felt honored to be a part of it. Not having any type of close family ties before them or memories to look back on, he hadn't known how good things could be until he found Liv.

But as he looked around the house, he couldn't help but feel an off-putting, eerie vibe. The hairs on the back of Bruce's neck were standing up—and the scariest part was he knew exactly why.

THE HOUSE THAT NO ONE WANTED

"How many fucking people died in this house?" Bruce asked, stretching out on the bed.

"Bruce, no!" Liv said, buttoning up her nightgown. "We agreed not to bring it up while we're staying here. You know it creeps me out."

"Creeps me out too . . ." Bruce made a stoic face.

A few whimpers came from the cage sitting on the floor.

"Spud," Liv said, "be a good boy for us and go to bed, please."

The normally cheerful dachshund's tail didn't give its usual wag in response.

"What's your problem?" Liv stuck her fingers through the cage, trying her best to comfort the puppy.

"Probably just doesn't like staying in this place," Bruce said. "Can you blame him?"

"It's okay, sweetie," Liv whispered to Spud.

"I mean, why would your mother sign up for this?"

"I told you before—she wants to own something." Liv joined him on the bed. "This is the only place close enough to our house that was even remotely in her price range."

"Well, yeah . . . when an entire sex cult commits suicide in the same house, that'll definitely trigger a discount."

Liv huffed, annoyed he was bringing it up again.

"But how the hell is she going to sleep here knowing that?" Bruce continued. "How are *we* going to sleep here knowing that?"

"You know she's always been terrified of being put in a nursing home. She's been telling me that ever since I graduated from high school. I think owning a house is her way of making her feel like that won't happen."

"Afraid of a nursing home?" Bruce scoffed. "Compared to the history of this goddamn place? She's got a bum ticker too . . . she'd be better off having help close by. I mean right down the hall. You don't think her coming here is just a little bit weird?"

"I never said that. It's super weird . . . but it's what she wants." Liv looked at him and smiled. "And when a woman knows what she wants, there's no stopping her."

Liv winked at Bruce, remembering all the reasons why she fell for him. The attention he showered her with was so genuine—never forced. He just had this way of making her feel like she was the only person on the planet.

Liv had always been so confident. Growing up, she was never afraid of the spotlight. A two-sport athlete—softball and track—she was accustomed to challenges. She'd never let a problem get the better of her. Her attitude was just as fiery as her beautiful locks.

Only recently, having put on some weight, had Liv ever shown a chink in her confidence. But Bruce was so sweet about it. He constantly reassured her of all the reasons he'd married her, always going out of his way to make her feel not just loved but adored.

"You know what else is weird?" Bruce asked.

Liv didn't answer him, instead opting to entertain herself with her phone. While she was hoping he wouldn't keep on with the creepy conversation, she wasn't about to hold her breath. Just sleeping in the house for the few days while they helped her mother unpack was unsettling enough.

Don't get all in your head about it, she thought.

Whenever she dwelled on the paranormal for too long, she ended up spooking herself. But whether she liked it or not, Bruce was going to be Bruce. With all the good he brought to the table, there was a joker side that loved to poke fun and mess around.

"In the news, they said it was a mass hanging. Up until I read that, I'd never heard of such a thing. It also said they did it in the basement . . . together. I can't remember how many there were exactly, but I know it was at least double digits. That's a lot of fucking people. I mean, can you imagine, walking in and seeing that many bodies hanging?"

Liv scrolled on her device. "I'd rather not."

"They said it was autoerotic asphyxiation . . ."

While she wasn't eager to talk about it, the wording did make her ears perk up. "What's that?"

Bruce raised his eyebrows. "It's when people, like, choke themselves or cut off their air supply so they can cum really hard. Supposedly it gives you some kind of mega orgasm or something. From what it said, I guess they all believed that, in combination with their rituals, the orgasm would be so intense that it would allow them to transcend worlds, or some shit."

Liv scrunched her nose. "Yuck."

"I mean, they were literally just describing what dying is." Bruce snickered. "What a bunch of morons." He turned to Liv. "But hey, don't knock it till you try it." He reached over and playfully wrapped his fingers around her throat.

"Hey!" Liv yelled. "Get the hell off me!"

The goofy grin on Bruce's face was priceless. Waggling his eyebrow, he jokingly said, "Aw, c'mon, babe. What's that saying . . . When in Rome?"

"No," she said with a giggle.

Bruce continued to grab Liv before pulling her in close. Their mini–wrestling match ended as he closed in and planted his lips on hers for a tender, loving kiss.

THE MOTHER OF BLISS

Dustin turned from Michael J. Fox riding his skateboard on the TV toward the quiet snore whistling from Alice's mouth. The room was dark aside from the flickering glow of the screen. Stretching his arms, Dustin yawned and adjusted his position on the couch.

As he rested his eyes, a faint popping noise from behind him caught his attention. He peeked over the back of the couch. Outside of the living room, past the kitchen, a shadowy form stood near a door. The featureless figure held its fist against its palm, and the sound of cracking knuckles repeated.

"Dad?" Dustin whispered.

When he rubbed his eyes, he heard the groan of wood creaking and quickly refocused on the darkness. The figure was no longer there, but the door it had been standing next to was now open.

Curious, Dustin stood and made his way toward it.

When he reached the doorway, he found a staircase that led to the basement. A dull yellow light from below added just enough detail to make out the steps.

"Dustin," a female voice whispered.

His ears perked up.

"Come down here," the voice continued.

"Mom?" he asked, wearing a half smile.

"You've got to come . . . you've got to come and see this," the voice begged.

Grabbing hold of the railing, Dustin quietly descended the staircase. With each step closer, the aged wood cried. A strange excitement swirled in his stomach as he wondered what surprise his mother might have in store for him.

"What is it?" he asked, his curiosity only growing.

As he rounded the corner, he felt a cold gust of air trigger goosebumps on his exposed skin. Before Dustin had a chance to even see what lay ahead, the light disappeared. The darkness before him was absolute, like a blanket soaked in used motor oil. His eyes remained unadjusted as they sifted through the dark, searching for his mother.

"Mom?" he called, slightly louder.

"I could be," the voice said. "I'd love to be . . ."

As his eyes scanned the nothingness, Dustin started to see an outline. The sharp facial features, yellow eyes, and pale skin brightened the room ever so slightly, like a dimmer being slowly turned up. The woman wasn't his mother, but she seemed so happy to see him.

"Who are you?" Dustin asked.

"I'm a mother to many," the woman whispered, grinning even wider. "The Mother of Bliss."

As Dustin's eyes continued to adjust, he noticed another feature the woman bore that unsettled him. Her scalp was exposed—the whiteness of her bald head was eerie. Dustin had never seen a lady without hair before.

The woman rubbed her tongue against her top lip. "You seem like such a happy boy."

When Dustin looked at her, he felt sleepy. Fixated on her eyes, he watched as they continued to glow like mini suns before dulling, burning out, and turning pitch black.

"And you want to stay happy . . . don't you?" the woman asked.

Dustin stood in awe of the strange woman, unable to take his gaze off her.

"Don't you?!" she screamed.

"Dustin, are you down there?" Alice's voice came from the top of the stairs.

Frozen by the terror, he listened to his grandmother's footsteps as they descended the steps. When they reached the bottom, the lights came on.

A massive circular rope encompassed the room, stretching the length of the entire ceiling. With over a dozen nooses knotted, the interconnected mesh left each one separated by only a few feet.

Occupying all the loops were the necks of men and women. As they dangled, the sounds of choking and gagging echoed off the walls. Their white eyes oozed a yellow fluid, and as they stirred, the golden liquid rained from each of their mouths.

The chorus of gagging screeches was paired with the bass rumble of flesh drumming against flesh. As Dustin gazed upon the horde of pale bodies, their excitement was undeniable. The flailing figures masturbated feverishly, the maddening echo of their hands thudding against their genitals only growing louder with each manic stroke and slap.

Dustin wanted to scream, but nothing came out. From his peripheral, he saw his grandmother, mouth agape with terror, one hand clasping at her chest as she went crashing to the floor. As she fell into the center of the circle of hanging bodies, she twitched violently, a subtle hiss of air draining from her form like a deflating beachball.

Knees suddenly weakening, Dustin felt his legs give out. As he joined his grandmother on the floor, he mimicked her body spasms without control. The basement lights began to flicker along with the motion of their bodies, in sync with the rhythm of the masturbation.

As the collection of groaning bodies continued to choke and violently pleasure themselves, they seemed to reach a pinnacle.

A warm rain of fluid showered both Dustin and his grandmother. The slimy, translucent liquid burst from the tips of the men and exploded wildly in all directions around the slits of the women.

When Dustin's body finally slowed, so did the lights, dimming to a minimal glow. The boy lay stiff. A tingling sensation streamed through his entire body as he regained feeling in his extremities. Forcing himself to sit up, Dustin picked himself off the floor and regained his footing. Confusion swirled in his mind as he glanced at the massive projection of his shadow cast over the basement wall.

After a sudden blink of the lights, the strange woman with the extinguished eyes loomed before him again.

"There are few things in life better than the sound of someone choking," she whispered.

Her intense grin seemed to grow even sharper as she seductively bit her lip and turned toward the wall. Dustin and the woman stood in place, like statues, and watched as her shadow closed in on his.

YEARS

LATER

UNHAPPY BIRTHDAY

The supply closet was tight, but no one ever went in there until after hours. There were moments when Liv just needed to get away from everyone in the office. Oftentimes, she had trouble bottling her emotions and needed a place where she didn't have to wear her mask of normalcy.

Why? she wondered, looking down at the birthday envelope that had Dustin's name written on the front.

She'd discovered the card when sifting through her purse for her medication. His fourteenth birthday had been weeks prior. There was no reason why he would put a birthday card addressed to himself in her purse.

Looking up at the tiled ceiling, she shook her head.

Why can't he just be normal?

She'd been afraid to open it all day, sitting at her desk, stewing. Thinking about the horror show that her homelife had become while also wondering what it could possibly contain.

As she ran her finger along the edge of the card, the sound of the paper tearing made her tremble. She took a deep breath and pulled the contents out.

When her eyes found the front of the card, they started to gloss over. Created by many lines of colored pencil was a picture of a woman with red hair—eerily similar to hers. The rope wound around the woman's neck was tight enough to make her eyes bulge out of their sockets. In addition to the horrified expression on the woman's face, streams of drool and blood leaked from her mouth.

God, no . . .

She wiped tears from the side of her face and opened the card. The scribbles inside were even worse than the imagery on the front.

> *All I wanted for my birthday was for you to choke. For you to know what it's like to feel that tightness around your throat along with the wetness in your pants. It's so much better than you'd think.*
>
> *I wish you would trust me.*
>
> *I'm tired of everyone not trusting me. I'm tired of being ignored. I won't continue to allow it. If you were smart, you'd let me put my hands around your fat neck and squeeze. I'm not even strong enough to kill you—even though sometimes I wish I was. I just want to see you choke and struggle to breathe. To know what bliss feels like.*
>
> *Is that too much to ask?*
>
> *I don't think so. But it seems like you do. Why else would you have gotten me those stupid fucking video games for my birthday?*
>
> *You're not __my__ mother.*
>
> *Dustin*

The colors in the card were starting to run after being wet by several tears. Liv's face was red as she closed the vile card and quickly slipped it back into the envelope.

When will it stop? I can't keep doing this!

As Liv looked up, she noticed the clock on the wall.

I've got to get back . . . Just hold it together.

Getting up from the stool, she lifted her purse off the ground and wiped away the tears once again.

As she slipped out the door, she tried to close it as quietly as possible.

"Did they run out of toilet paper?" a joking voice asked.

When she turned to see her coworker Fredson Dennard smiling, she felt so embarrassed. Liv knew she must look a mess.

"I . . . no, I just needed a minute to myself," Liv said.

Fred furrowed his brow, clearly concerned by the sight of her. "Jeez, Liv, is everything okay?"

"What do you mean?" She straightened up, trying her best to gaslight him.

"You just . . . you look like you've been crying."

"I'm fine," she said, swinging her purse over her shoulder and nodding. "I'm always fine."

"You know, if there's something wrong, you can tell me. Sometimes it helps to talk about it."

"Thank you, Fred. But I've been talking for years, and it hasn't changed anything."

She thought about all the therapists, not only that she'd seen but the ones Dustin had seen. Liv had given up on several over the years and stopped taking Dustin to his after he coldly explained that he'd kill himself if he was ever forced to attend another session.

"Maybe you're just talking to the wrong people," Fred suggested.

"Maybe . . ." Liv looked at her watch and bit her lip. "I've gotta get back to my desk."

"Okay." Fred nodded and moved aside. "I hope everything works out."

"Thanks," Liv replied.

She made her way back to her desk and sat down. Opening the bottom drawer, she slid her handbag inside and paused. Next to the purse sat several bags of junk food. She eyeballed them for a moment before reaching inside and pulling out a king-size candy bar.

Exhaling, she shoved the bar inside her mouth and started to chew. The flavor and the motion of her jaw helped distract her from the horrible thoughts swirling inside her head.

Her eyes drifted to the picture on her desk. It was of Liv, Bruce, and Dustin, taken outside of a waterpark. She displayed that specific photo because it was back when Dustin was just a little boy, and it was the last picture she had of her son smiling.

DRIVE OF DREAD

As Bruce locked the door to Carnegie's, he took a deep breath. The shop felt more like home than the place he was heading. Inside these walls, the countless antiques were easy to get lost in—a most welcome distraction.

When he got inside his car, he hesitated to turn the key. He fantasized about pulling up to the parking lot exit and turning in the opposite direction. Just driving on the asphalt until he was thousands of miles away from them.

He reached into the console and extracted a bottle of pills. After fishing one out, he thought better of it and located a second pill.

Two's fine, he thought. *Just for today.*

The medication had been losing its bite. He felt like he needed more with each day he took it. It wasn't even so much a feeling as it was reality. Back when he was younger, he'd never imagined that he would be the kind of man who used medication as a crutch. But then again, he never could've foreseen the twisted day-to-day affairs he now had to deal with.

The worst part might have been not knowing what to expect. Sure, there were still some good days, but they were few and far between. No matter how many tablets he swallowed, that wasn't going to change what was happening around him.

The drive home in the evening was like torture. Normally, people look at their estimated time of arrival and are excited to reach the destination and relax. For Bruce, that wasn't the case. With each minute that dwindled, his blood pressure rose. His mind raced as he wondered what he was in store for that night.

Bruce put the pills in his mouth and took a sip from the flat soda bottle that had been sitting in his car. As he set the drink back down, something made him pause. The square picture of Spud, happy and wagging his tail, hanging from the rearview caught his eye.

Bruce forced a smile.

"At least I've got you."

Keying up the GPS, Bruce searched and selected a local pet store.

"You deserve to be spoiled."

He reversed, put the car in drive, and pulled out of the parking lot.

DINNER TWO WAYS

Dustin sucked on the corncob in a way that he knew would make both of his parents uncomfortable. After biting off and swallowing all the warm kernels, he'd inserted the bare, pointed edge of the pith into his mouth the long way.

As Liv watched him, her face was blanketed with many emotions. Disappointment, sadness, and fear were all quite ordinary expressions in this house.

"Dustin . . . please," Liv whispered.

Taking the cob out of his mouth, Dustin looked at Spud. The dog sat away from the table in the corner of the room. The dachshund watched him closely, emitting a subdued but steady growl.

As Dustin's eyes hung on the hound, he could feel the animal's anxiety rising. The tension in the room transferred through Dustin—he was the conduit.

The uneasiness became too much for the animal. A final whimper of worry escaped Spud before he stood on all fours and exited the kitchen in favor of the isolation that the living room offered.

Dustin started to snicker, taking pleasure in the animal's discomfort. But he quickly cut off his own giggle, gagging himself with the bare corncob again.

Liv stopped eating—her face held the same strain of discomfort as the dog before he'd left. Still, despite the absurd act unfolding before her, she hesitated to speak. But it didn't take long for the unpleasant choking noises to become unbearable.

"That's not a toy," Liv said.

Shrugging, Dustin turned toward his uneasy mother. He extracted the cob from his mouth and held it up, the drool sliming down over his hand.

"But it looks like one, doesn't it?" Dustin asked.

His eyes bounced to his father. Bruce sat silently, as if in his own world. Carving into the moist cut of beef on his plate aggressively, he clenched his teeth, desperate to ignore their conversation.

Dustin understood his father preferred to be detached from the family. The man lived inside his mind—very much in the same way a part of Dustin did. The enthusiasm with which Bruce sliced into the bleeding meat made Dustin imagine his dad might be fantasizing about cutting into his teenage body, putting an abrupt and violent end to the constant worry, stress, and heartache. There would be no more questions, no need to ponder or pray. It would finally be finished.

Dustin grinned gleefully, excited by the dark idea. While he would have preferred being strangled to death, maybe if Bruce stabbed him in the right places, he could choke to death on his own blood.

As he held the pointed cob in front of him, a substantial pearl of spit oozed from the tip onto his plate. He stared at the corn, admiring the shape, and his smile widened as fast as the bloody cut being slashed into Bruce's steak.

"Actually, it looks just like the toys in your dresser," Dustin said, turning to Liv.

Dustin liked making eye contact with his mother when he said such things. The more uncomfortable she was, the better. The dread poured from her face like water from a busted pipe, leaving her paralyzed.

"You know," he continued, gesturing to Bruce, "the toys you have to fuck yourself with now . . . since he won't anymore."

Bruce stopped eating and stared blankly at the cabinet across from the table, the devastation inside his shaky pupils looking like his brain had just been microwaved. It was the kind of look seen inside patients in mental institutions, not nice upper-class homes.

As Liv's eyes started to well, Dustin's father carefully set his fork down.

Without saying a word, Bruce stood from the table, left what remained of his food, and headed for the stairs.

"But this tastes *so* much better," Dustin said.

Bruce paused in front of the staircase, cheeks blushing, hands trembling, clearly in deep thought.

Dustin licked at the tip again as if to simulate preparing for oral sex. "I can understand why he stopped fucking you. Since your toys taste like pimple pus, then you must too."

Tears beaded and rolled down Liv's face as she stared ahead, speechless. Dustin kept his eyes on his mother, but in his peripheral, he watched Bruce walk up the stairs.

"Please . . ." Liv whispered, more tears racing down her face. "Please, just stop . . ."

Dustin ignored her, chuckling. The agony radiating off his mother was so satisfying.

"I liked it better *before* you started using those things so much," Dustin continued. "I used to like sneaking up to your bedroom door and listening to you and Dad have sex. I liked listening to you choke when you had his cock in your throat. Do you remember that?"

Liv didn't respond. She just kept her head down, biting her lip hard.

"Do you remember?!" Dustin screamed, slamming his fist against the table so hard that it caused the silverware to clatter.

"Y-yes," she whispered.

"Good."

Dustin felt a sense of power and relief when she obeyed him. When he could see the fear he produced at work, manipulating her like a terrified meat puppet.

Lip quivering, Liv wiped a tear away, her face begging for an answer. "Why do you always have to say such horrible things?" she asked.

"Because . . . I know it hurts you when I do," he whispered, looking back at the cob in his hand.

Adjusting the pith, Dustin plunged it into his throat again but this time deeper than before. When the rough tip scratched at his uvula, it triggered a violent lurch.

Instantly, a flood of watery mashed potatoes, chunky corn kernels, and bits of beef erupted from his mouth. The milky vomit hailed over the remaining food on Dustin's plate, creating what looked like a steaming pile of mashed soup.

Liv held her hands over her face, sobbing hysterically. Despite what was happening, she remained submissive, fearful, and obedient.

"I-I just want it to stop," she cried. "Why can't it stop?"

Some days, when Dustin made such scenes, his mother would crack. The dread would loom over her before crashing down like a thousand-pound weight had just been dropped. Other days, she had a little more fight. Other days, she might've screamed at him. But as she sat before him in that instant, broken and sobbing, he knew that he'd struck a nerve.

Dustin grinned, reaching for the puke-covered spoon at the side of his plate. He always enjoyed it when she talked to God or whoever she did in moments of despair. The rush of dopamine such desperation generated was incomparable to most anything else his blooming brain could register. Suddenly, he felt stronger—more alive.

Maneuvering the utensil, Dustin knocked the gooey cob out of the way and scooped up a spoonful of the sludge he'd just regurgitated. It was still nice and warm when he dumped it back into his mouth. Laughing, he started to chew the partially digested clumps for the second time.

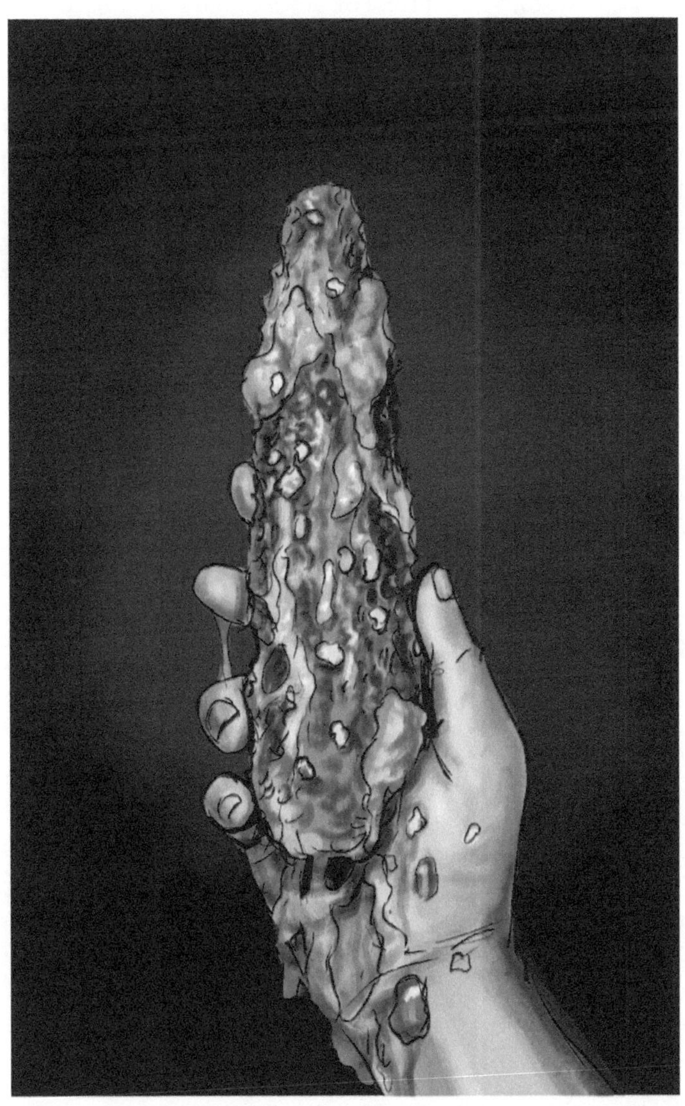

"I can't take it anymore," Liv whimpered. Her full-on breakdown triggered a rope of drool to fall from her mouth onto her plate. "It has to stop . . . I-I *need* it to stop."

As Dustin swallowed the wad of vomit, he turned back to his mother. "Stop?" He let out a sinister giggle. "We've only just begun."

THE TINIEST DETAIL

Justine Katz made sure to convey her excitement when she welcomed Russell Stevens and his son, Jimmy, over the threshold and into the building. She knew if Russell was going to entrust the Carter School with his child's future and development, then she would need to ensure that Mr. Stevens felt comfortable with not only her attitude but also her management style, the facility, and the other personnel.

"Welcome," Justine said. "I'm so glad we've finally got you here for a tour."

"Thank you," Russell said with a nod. "We're excited too."

The man was on the taller side, with a stout and muscular frame. Justine wasn't surprised by his appearance—when they had initially discussed his son's potential enrollment, he'd told her over the phone that he was a single father currently working in the construction industry.

Jimmy, on the other hand, was much different. The opposite of his father's masculine posture, the boy stood hunched over, swaying side to side. His dad's confidence clearly wasn't genetic. The boy looked like he wasn't comfortable in his own skin. Rubbing his sweaty hands nervously and chewing his lip, Jimmy harbored an expression of profound worry, looking as though he were being led to the gas chamber rather than touring a school.

"Sweetie, it's okay," Justine said, squatting closer to his face and placing her hand over her heart. "I promise you, there's nothing to be nervous about. This is a fun place filled with kind people." She winked at him. "You're going to fit right in."

"See, nothing to worry about, Son." Russell squeezed his boy's shoulders gently. "You're gonna be just fine."

As they made their way down the hall, Justine pointed out the different classrooms.

"This is most likely where you'd be learning, if you decided to join us," Justine said, signaling to a closed door on the left.

Russell picked up his son, and they both peered through the sliver of glass on the door. "Looks pretty good, bud. What do you think?"

Jimmy nodded, but his brow remained wrinkled.

Russell's eye was caught by a red door at the opposite end of the hall. Pointing toward it, he looked back at Justine. "What's that?"

"That's the Maximum Care wing," Justine said. "It's an area for children with the deepest needs. It's the smallest section of our school and the only part that's segregated— only for safety purposes, of course."

She could tell by the look on Russell's face that just her explanation alone terrified him.

"I see," Russell said.

"Actually, follow me." Justine waved. "I'd like to show you something."

Russell furrowed his brow. "Is it safe to—?"

"We're not actually going inside," she said. "The door requires a keycard entry, so there is nothing to fear. But I think this will put you at ease."

As Russell started to walk, Justine stopped him.

"Maybe let Jimmy stay here by himself for a moment, just so we can have a quick word."

"Oh, sure," Russell said. "Just hang here a second. Okay, Jimbo?"

"Sh-sh-sure, Dad," Jimmy said.

As Justine guided him down the hall, Russell kept an eye on his son from afar. They stopped at the wall beside the red door, in front of a framed picture of a teenage girl. The young lady was grinning from ear to ear.

"This is Kelsey Emit—one of our former students in the Extreme Care wing," Justine said.

"Former?"

"Yes. There's a reason her picture's on the wall. After receiving treatment here, Kelsey no longer requires a special-needs curriculum. Just a short time ago, she transitioned from the Carter School to a local public school. She's a shining example of the hard work our staff does here."

Russell looked back at Jimmy, seemingly hoping that the same could be in the cards for his boy. "That's incredible."

"I agree, but it's really not the *most* incredible part of her story . . ."

Russell returned his gaze to her. "Really?"

"You can only appreciate Kelsey's metamorphosis if you know what she evolved from."

He leaned in, waiting for her to spill the beans.

"Kelsey," Justine continued, "was in a mental institution for three years before arriving at our school." She turned from the picture to face Russell. "She was committed after a walk with her sister, during which Kelsey decided she wanted to cut off a piece of her sister's breast."

Russell's eyes widened. "Why?"

"She wanted to eat it. And she did. Well . . . most of it."

"My God."

"I apologize to have to be so graphic," Justine said. "But again, this wing of the school is always locked down and uses an entirely separate exit and entrance. So from a safety perspective, there's nothing to worry about. I only wanted to share the extreme nature of the story with you so that you understand what a colossal task normalizing Kelsey and re-acclimating her into society was. But it's a task we tackled as a team and couldn't be more proud of."

"That's . . . pretty insane."

"A boy like Jimmy, with issues not even remotely close to what Kelsey's were, should be a far easier undertaking. We look forward to working with him."

Russell looked back at his son with what looked like a mixture of adoration and anxiety. He seemed like the type of father who wanted to always do what was best for his boy.

"That would be . . ."

"A relief?" Justine finished for him.

Russell nodded, clearly trying to contain his emotion. She could see the weight he carried on his shoulders. Justine had him right where she wanted him.

"Wonderful." She grinned. "Now, I'd love to show you around the rest of the school. I think you and Jimmy will be very excited."

Guiding them onward, she showed Russell and Jimmy the lunch hall and where the restrooms were located. The inside of the school was state of the art, filled with the most modern accommodations, extravagant furniture, and technology.

They reached the outdoor recess yard, the landscaping of which was a sight to marvel. Everything was meticulously cared for, the idea being that anyone who saw it would think that if they took that much care of the facility, the attention to those enrolled would easily match it.

Looping around, they finally made their way into the gymnasium. The class inside the gym played various games while several teachers watched over the group. Some of the children with learning disabilities were rambunctious, so the extra help was always good to have on hand.

"As you can see"—Justine pointed to her peers—"we always have several teachers on hand when the kids are doing *anything* physical. Exercise is important, but we want to ensure we're always cultivating a safe environment for our kids."

Jimmy started biting his fingernail, looking even more worried as he watched the kids zip around the gym, throw balls, and scream wildly.

Russell studied his son carefully. Jimmy's gaze drifted off the rowdy kids, to a red-haired boy sitting on one of the bleachers. The boy seemed focused on his drawing as he used a colored pencil to bring it to life.

"This is great," Russell said, taking a half step back and whispering into Justine's ear. "But as much as I'd like him to be more . . . open . . . right now Jimmy's not really into sports or activities like these. It's kind of a trigger for his anxiety, actually. Are there other—?"

"Do you like my drawing?" Dustin asked, holding his pad up for Jimmy to see.

Justine's eyes darted to the boy who'd slyly crept over from the bleachers and inspected his pencil drawing. The image depicted a small boy holding what looked like a flame in one of his hands. But the part of the illustration that truly made her eyes widen was the massive shadow bleeding off the boy's body. The dark outline projected on the wall was several times what she would've imagined a normal shadow to be.

"Th-th-that's so c-cool!" Jimmy said, eyes lighting up as he stuttered with excitement.

Dustin smiled and pointed to the bleachers where his colored pencils remained. "I have more pencils if you wanna help me color it in!"

Looking back at his father, Jimmy's eyes begged before he did. "P-p-please, Dad! P-please!"

Russell looked at Justine.

"Oh, it's fine by me," she said with a smile.

"Have fun," Russell said.

"Thanks, Dad!" Jimmy yelled.

"Thank Ms. Katz. She gave the okay."

"Thank you, M-M-Ms. Katz."

Her smile only grew. "You're very welcome, Jimmy."

As the boys took off toward the bleachers, Russell seemed relieved by what he saw. Justine felt like she could see a dark cloud clearing out from above his head. It was something she recognized with most of the parents who decided to choose the Carter School for their children.

They were all just looking for a way to ease their worries. But the glossiness in Russell's eyes wasn't something that was typical. It was different.

"Is everything all right?" Justine asked.

"Yeah." It sounded like Russell was trying his best to hold back tears. "It's just . . . since he lost his mom, it's been really hard for him. To see him excited like that . . . to see him make a friend so easily . . . It just means a lot to me."

Justine put her hand on his shoulder. "I'm sorry you've both had to experience loss. I give you my word, I'm going to keep an eye on him and make sure he acclimates just fine."

"Thank you so much," Russell whispered.

"Of course."

As they watched the children around them, Justine continued to try to let him know he was making the right decision.

"In a school with many different—and some challenging—personalities, oftentimes it's the tiniest details that are the most important. Rest assured, I'm here for all my kids. And I'm paying attention to *all* the details."

Russell nodded.

Justine looked at Dustin and Jimmy sitting gleefully in the distance. With the picture Dustin had drawn still fresh in her mind, it was impossible for her eyes not to drift. As the sun shone through the windows at the top of the gym, Dustin's shadow stretched, spreading out around him like an abstract painting.

SACRIFICE

Liv removed the last sex toy from the dresser, arm shaking as she quickly dropped it into the black garbage bag. She'd thought she'd properly hidden them, but the dinner table conversation the prior evening dispelled that notion. Dustin was a lot of things, but she'd never known him to be a snoop. On top of everything else, his newfound nosiness would be another characteristic of his troubling personality she'd have to constantly be aware of.

Stay alert, Liv thought.

The toys had been in her underwear drawer, hidden in a discreet box, buried under a pile of seldom-used lingerie. She stared at the sexy garments, eyes glossing over, subtly shaking her head.

As she listened to the toy slide against the bag, her focus shifted. The thought of Dustin—her own son—touching and sucking on them made her gag. One of the few selfish pleasures that remained in her life would have to be exiled. Still, it almost didn't even faze her—it wasn't the first time she'd sacrificed for the sake of her family, and it most likely wouldn't be the last. Shuddering, she thought again about the nastiness at the dinner table. She'd do anything not to feel that way again, but such things were beyond her control.

Where does he get these sick ideas?

She'd done everything she could to raise him right—at least that's what she believed. All those years ago, she'd sat stroking her rotund stomach, envisioning a tiny angel was set to squeeze its way out of her body. But the boy who had rattled off such vile obscenities so freely over dinner didn't remotely resemble the one she'd imagined. This led her to constantly question everything. Including her own role in his devolution.

Was it . . . something I did? Was it me?

It was an unanswerable question. Not a single one of the slew of doctors who'd evaluated Dustin over the years had found anything in her parenting or Bruce's that they viewed as a major contributing factor to his extreme behavior. In *all* their professional opinions, the boy was stricken with some kind of mental anomaly that no one could quite seem to put their finger on with any confidence.

They'd already tried every suggestion offered to them. Every medication, every counselor, and every traditional or radical behavioral therapy they came across. But nothing worked. And with each year that went by, Dustin remained in the same mold. Until so much time had passed that both Liv and Bruce were defeated. Beaten to the ground by the two-punch of their own parental failures and Dustin's perverse relentlessness.

They walked on eggshells, constantly awaiting the next outburst or incident they'd undoubtedly be tasked with handling. They didn't have the fight any longer. It was why Bruce had left when Dustin made the comments at the dinner table, and why Liv had just sobbed.

There was no question about who was running their family—Dustin was the dominant presence. A fourteen-year-old boy was the authority of their household.

Liv lifted the garbage bag and walked toward the dresser. She allowed some spit to collect inside her mouth as she opened her pillbox.

I can't do it alone.

She tossed a pill into her mouth and swallowed it down. Depression and anxiety were always lurking, and sometimes a little pick-me-up was required to get through her days. Especially with an uncomfortable task like the one at hand.

Glancing over, her eyes found the several pill bottles collected on Bruce's side of the dresser. They were both in the same boat—leveraging a chemical escape to stay sane. The fact her husband was also being prescribed medication made Liv feel slightly better. She wasn't the weaker parent—they were both weak. While that still wasn't ideal for their situation, it felt good not to be alone. They'd grown apart, yes, but at least they still had that much in common.

Moving on to the door, she turned the knob and looked down the hallway at Dustin's room. His door remained closed, an eerie quietness haunting the space around it.

The silence itself was concerning—not as much as his disgusting behavior, but still bizarre. It was another odd-shaped puzzle piece amongst a vast collection of red flags. He didn't act like a child. It was like he was surrounded by a sinister void—the absence of adolescence.

Most any other child would be bouncing off the walls at his age. Playing games, watching television, out with their friends—things Liv had done when she was a kid. But that wasn't the case for Dustin. It was either chaos or silence.

If only he could just find a friend . . . or pick a hobby or play a sport. If only he had something. Anything. *Maybe he just hasn't had enough time at the new school?*

The questions she asked herself were designed to keep her hopeful. Dustin had been kicked out of his prior school for spitting on his teacher and threatening her. While she didn't consider her son special-needs necessarily, he most definitely had severe behavioral issues and deeply concerning outbursts.

The Carter School seemed like a good fit. The principal—Ms. Katz—was nice enough. The way she'd explained it to Liv and Bruce, the school was for kids from all walks of life. They tried their best to make the children who might have a more turbulent history not feel like outsiders.

While children with learning disabilities were being taught separately from other kids dealing with emotional outbursts and anger, none of them would be completely isolated in their groups. Ms. Katz had explained that it was part of her job to ensure that all the kids dealing with more extreme emotional issues also figured out how to acclimate to the larger group, and ensured there would be social events and situations designed so everyone could feel included.

Liv had been worried at first. After Dustin's prior expulsion, there weren't many other schools in the area that would be able to accommodate his special needs. So after the first few months had passed without incident, Liv was ecstatic.

Still, Dustin hadn't changed. The incidents she'd witnessed firsthand revealed that much. Her hopefulness was dotted with countless hints of confusion. Since their home-life hadn't changed, she considered the nagging notion that continued to rise to the surface: It wasn't Ms. Katz or the school that had made Dustin refrain from his outbursts. That was a decision on Dustin's part.

Why the inconsistency?

She didn't want to dwell on it any longer. It was great to know there weren't any issues at school. But after so much cyclical negativity and tension, she couldn't help herself.

Just enjoy it while it lasts.

Liv flipped the light switch on and quickly made her way down the stairs as she tied off the garbage bag, eager to be rid of its contents. Opening the front door, Liv swiftly approached the trashcan. She lifted the lid and threw the bag inside before slamming it shut. When she turned back toward the house, through the window, she saw Bruce sitting in his office.

Bruce stared at his computer with a pair of headphones clamped over his ears. There was a look of excitement twinkling in his eyes—a look that left Liv dejected and feeling forlorn.

He hadn't looked at her with such interest in some time. Bruce normally wasn't in bed until hours after she set her head on her pillow. That truth made her heart ache.

Liv reentered the house and approached the door to his office. She knocked three times and turned the handle. Even when she appeared in the doorway, he didn't take notice of her. He remained keyed in on whatever was on the screen.

"Hey," Liv said.

There was no response.

Liv walked in closer, finally causing Bruce to twitch. A look of surprise transitioned to annoyance as he slid the headphones off.

"Don't you knock?"

Liv's posture folded inward as a feeling of shame overcame her. "I—I did . . . Maybe you couldn't hear with your headpho—"

"I'm trying to finish up some stuff for work."

She knew he was lying. Certainly, Bruce was passionate about Carnegie's, but the passion she'd witnessed in his eyes was not the platonic sort.

Maybe it's still work-related . . . Is he fucking a coworker? Maybe a clerk or one of the appraisers? Maybe a customer?

"Okay . . ." Liv whispered defeatedly. "I'm going upstairs. I'll see you in a bit."

"It . . ." Bruce paused, the aggravation seeming to drain out of his face. He furrowed his brow and tapped his fingers against the desk. It was like he was holding back, trying to figure out the words he wanted to use. He nodded and fixed his gaze back on the computer screen. "It shouldn't be too much longer."

As Liv watched him lift the headphones back over his ears again, a hollowness filled her soul. There were no more hugs and kisses, no more goodnights, no more I-love-yous. There was nothing except for the wedge of darkness and vitriol between them that they'd allowed Dustin to create.

The boat they shared had sunk long ago. They'd crashed into an unforgiving iceberg of issues, only to be left drowning in their own dread. Floating helplessly, side by side, and all the while not uttering a single word of encouragement to each other.

She wanted to say something to him—to ask why things couldn't be like they had been before. But Bruce was already gone. Sucked back into the computer screen, and God only knew how long that would last.

Closing the office door, she turned and looked up, suddenly noticing the lights in the hallway had been switched off. In the faint moonlight, at the top of the staircase, she saw the silhouette of a tall person, their head round and bald.

As she gawked in horror at the dark figure, a guttural shriek escaped her. She looked toward Bruce's office, reaching for the door, before bouncing her attention back to the top of the stairs. The creepy outline from moments ago was no longer there. Instead of opening Bruce's door, she reached for the light switch.

The stairs and hallway were illuminated, but she saw nothing. Shaking her head, Liv felt the terror slowly dissipate.

Damn meds. The side effects never stop . . .

Not only was there a battle going on in the house between Liv's entire family, but there was another battle that was hidden. The one raging in her own mind. Seeing strange things occasionally had become the norm. Liv couldn't be sure if it was the stress of Dustin's eccentric lies and sinister behavior that had helped foster such occurrences, or maybe the medication she was now a subscriber to as a result of them. It was probably a combination of the two.

It's fine.

It wasn't.

Everything's fine. Just go to bed.

Bothering Bruce again wasn't an option she wanted to pursue. With the number of abnormal happenings they dealt with on a daily basis, there was no room to throw her personal ones into the mix.

As Liv crept up the staircase, she held her breath. Part of her wondered if the thing she'd seen might just reappear when she reached the top. She pictured the dark figure pushing her and triggering a violent backward tumble.

The fictitious sound of her neck snapping was a dark fantasy that she found some peace in.

It would all be over at last . . . No more pressure. No more fear. Just nothing . . .

Cautiously climbing the stairs, Liv made it to the top without incident. But as she turned to the door of her bedroom, she was startled once again. Dustin stood, an unsettling mask of emotionlessness suffocating his freckled face. He was just waiting. Liv didn't shriek aloud this time, but she did inside.

"Hey, Mom," Dustin said.

Her eyes grew wide.

He doesn't usually call me Mom. He must want something.

"Dustin . . . it's late. Shouldn't you be in bed?"

He nodded. "But I wanted to ask you something before I go to sleep."

Liv bit her lip and then released it. "Okay . . .?"

"Can Jimmy Stevens sleep over this weekend?"

The request came out of left field. Liv shook her head, both surprised and confused. "Who's Jimmy Stevens?"

Dustin's eyes were glazed over and dark. "My friend."

GUYS' NIGHT

Spud's tail wagged happily as Bruce dropped a fresh bone in front of him. He got down on his knees and leaned in close, lovingly petting the dog. There were few things Bruce enjoyed more than isolating himself with Spud. It didn't happen much, but he always knew exactly what he was in for when it did. The locked office door made him feel cozy and safe. He imagined it did the same for Spud.

"That's right," Bruce said, nuzzling his nose against Spud's side. "Tonight's guys' night. That's why Daddy got a special new bone for his favorite puppy."

As he played with the dog, Bruce felt some of his anxiety start to subside. While he still called Spud a puppy, he was far from a spring chicken. Gray in the mouth, the faithful pet had undoubtedly aged faster from the sheer stress of living in their turbulent household.

"You're always there for me, aren't you, buddy?"

Bruce rubbed the dog's head once more, watching the excitement in Spud's body language as he gnawed on the bone. Moving past his work desk, Bruce eyed the recliner beside the window in the corner of the room. Some beers, his phone, a Zippo, and a poorly rolled joint lay on the small table beside the luxury seat.

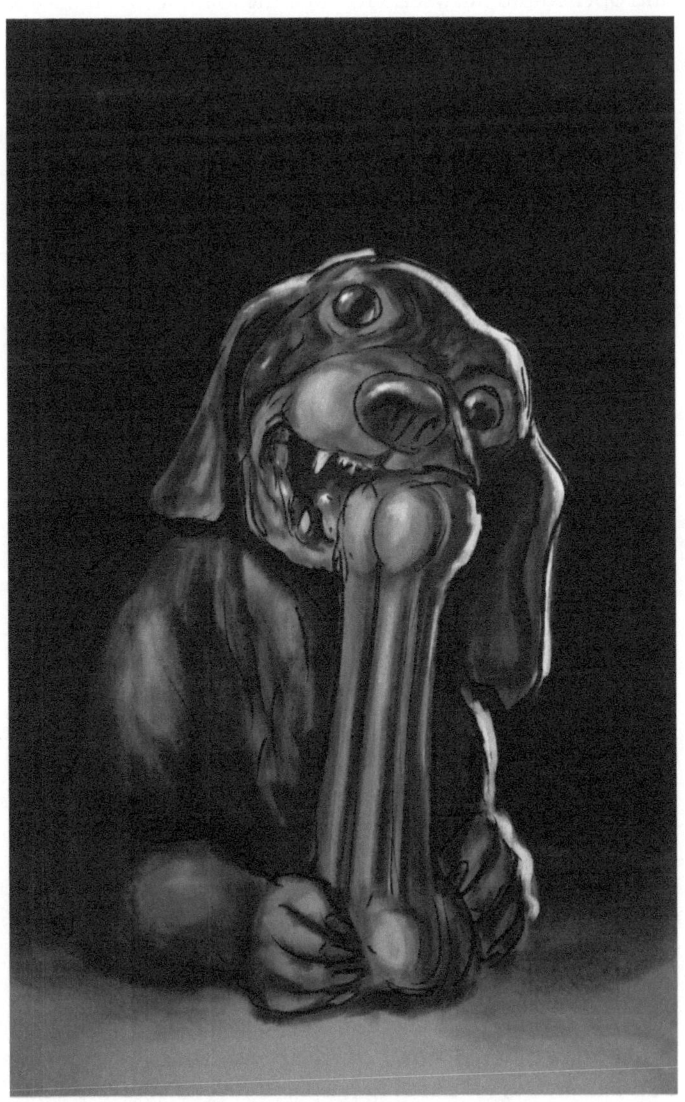

Plopping down, Bruce grabbed his phone with one hand and opened the browser. He stuck the joint between his lips and looked down at the screen. Opening the window, he exhaled out his nose, trying his best to relax. The toned chick in the yoga pants on his phone triggered a partial erection to inflate his jogging pants.

She's bad, he thought.

Once the window was open, Bruce put his phone down on the sill. He plucked the joint from his lips and looked at it. The thing was a monstrosity—it looked like it was rolled by someone with Parkinson's disease.

What the hell was I thinking? I should've just gotten a few of those pre-rolled ones.

He continued to gawk at the ugly joint, shaking his head in aggravation. The spliff was about as loose as the screws in Dustin's head.

Don't think about him right now. This is your *time.*

Weed wasn't usually Bruce's thing, but lately, he'd found himself trending outside of his norms. At Carnegie's, one of the antique appraisers he worked with had mentioned how getting high was much different now. How all the weed was categorized into different strains and how the people at the bud boutiques explained in great detail what kind of vibe each one fosters.

The idea of purchasing weed was still weird to him. He was from an era when getting caught buying, carrying, smoking, or selling usually meant jail time.

Times have changed.

He looked down at the tiny canister the weed came in and laughed. There was a silly picture of a red-eyed monkey above a logo that read *Ape Shit.*

The appraiser had inadvertently sold him on smoking cannabis again. Accessing it was easy enough now, and after Bruce remembered how, when he was younger, smoking bud had always loosened him up and helped alleviate whatever tension he was dealing with, he figured it couldn't hurt to give it a try.

After all, with Liv watching over Dustin and his new friend sleeping over, Bruce needed to make the most out of his alone time. It wasn't often that he knew the rest of his family would be completely occupied.

Toying with the joint, Bruce realized he was both excited and nervous to smoke again. Excited at the potential of escaping the turmoil that lay beyond the locked door of his office, and nervous about how the marijuana might clash with his medication—not to mention adding a few beers to the equation.

Fuck it. I need this.

Bruce put the joint back between his lips, raised the lighter, and set it ablaze. The Zippo was a wedding gift from Liv—one he'd forgotten about. It had been stored away carefully until he'd stumbled across it looking for a hiding spot for his weed.

Gazing down upon the shiny brass, Bruce thought about Liv. They were so different back when she had given it to him. If that version of Liv and Bruce stood side by side with them now, they would be unrecognizable.

Jesus . . . what the hell happened to us?

He didn't know why he'd even bothered to ask himself the question—he damn well knew the answer. But again, he wasn't trying to think about Dustin. Not tonight. As the thought haunted his mind, he took a deep pull from the joint.

His inhalation was quickly stunted by a cough.

Eyes starting to water, Bruce calmed his fit and set the joint down in the ashtray. His lungs hadn't felt the harshness of smoke for some time. Reaching for the semi-cold beer, he took a swig and looked out the window into the dark woods that surrounded their house.

Bruce's finger slowly grazed over the initials *B.H.* etched into the side of the lighter. The individual who the initials belonged to—Braxton Hanover—was long gone. Hanover was a military general who'd gotten that particular Zippo the very first year of the lighter company's inception.

Still works like a charm.

Liv of course gifted him the item on account of Bruce being a dealer and his overall adoration for antiques. He was one of the rare people who was able to make an earnest living doing what he loved more than anything.

The lighter excited him initially because the general happened to have the same initials as Bruce. In addition to the lucky coincidence, he knew it would hit the hundred-year mark and therefore become a true antique within his lifetime.

But in that moment, even more important than the lighter's value was its power.

A fearless military man had held that very same flame. The lighter had guided General Hanover through the bleak darkness of war. Maybe it could do the same for Bruce. Maybe the ghosts of the past could somehow help Bruce battle through the familial warfare he'd been caught in the middle of.

Yeah, right.

Bruce looked back at Spud, who had already chewed through a decent chunk of his fresh bone. He might've been old, but his teeth still worked and his jaw and bite remained powerful.

At least I've got you.

Picking up the smoldering joint, Bruce took a controlled drag this time. The weed tasted so much better than the garbage pot he used to smoke back in the day. With his tastebuds enticed, he felt his mouth form a grin.

Eyes drifting to the photo on the wall, Bruce saw himself smiling. But the smile on his face in the picture and the one he felt in real time were completely different. With Liv and Dustin flanking him in the photo, he knew the emotion captured that day was a façade. The photo shoot was just one of the many things they did as a family so they didn't feel like total freaks.

We could've been fine . . .

Bruce glared at Dustin's frowning, freckled face. Just the sight of him made his skin crawl.

. . . if it wasn't for him.

It was easy for Bruce to be pessimistic—that was all he'd known for many years. But when he hit the weed again, along with the smoke, a little hope filled his torso.

He is *having a sleepover . . .*

That was something Bruce hadn't seen coming. Dustin had *never* had any friends. This whole hangout had come out of nowhere, but he was glad it was happening. Maybe his son was finally turning over a new leaf. Maybe that school was everything it claimed to be. Maybe after all the chaos, depression, and torture he'd put them through, things were finally going to change into the kind of life Bruce and Liv had imagined on their wedding day all those years ago.

Then he thought about the dinner table conversation a few nights prior and shook his head.

Nah. No fucking way.

PLAYING GAMES

Dustin watched Jimmy closely as he sat in the gaming chair positioned in front of the television. The download bar on the screen was only filled about ten percent of the way. The other boy's leg bobbed up and down as he eagerly waited for the game to finish downloading.

Jimmy turned from the screen to Dustin. "I-I thought y-y-you said you already d-downloaded it . . ."

"Yeah, that's what I told you," Dustin replied, opening the nightstand drawer on the far side of his bed.

Jimmy exhaled, huffing with agitation.

Dustin gazed into the drawer, remembering when he'd met Jimmy. He was different than the other more erratic kids Dustin was stuck in the classroom with at school. He was smart enough to realize that Jimmy had different struggles, ones that weren't so aggressive in nature.

Jimmy spoke with a stutter or sometimes a slur, while other times he had trouble verbalizing his ideas altogether. Unless he was engaged in some kind of activity, his mind was kind of all over the place. Dustin figured that was why he was so distracted now—he would've been entranced if the video game was ready, but instead, he was acting like a lost child.

While Dustin wasn't in the same class as Jimmy, their chance encounter in the gym had allowed them to form an unlikely friendship. Their school was filled with all different types of kids, and finally, Dustin was able to meet the type of person he'd been waiting for—quiet, odd, calm, timid, depressed, and unathletic. There had been others he'd noticed, but at school, despite his good behavior, Dustin's opportunities had been scarce.

The last school he'd attended hadn't had anyone truly to his liking. That was why he'd made the decision to leave. When he'd told his teacher he'd love to watch her choke to death, Dustin had enjoyed watching the shock jolt her expression. It was like she'd been electrocuted by a live wire. But when he followed that up by spitting between her legs, her shock turned to mortification. While the interaction had given him some pleasure, it wasn't exactly the kind he'd been chasing.

"Is th-that yours?" Jimmy asked, pointing to the wooden hockey stick in the corner of the room. "I-I don't like sports . . . I th-th-thought you didn't e-either."

"I don't," Dustin said. "It was a gift to try and get me more involved in sports. But it didn't work."

Jimmy turned back to the download bar on the screen, still taking its sweet time. "This is taking f-f-forever."

"We're almost there," Dustin replied. "Shouldn't be too much longer . . ."

"But I w-w-wanna play n-*now* . . ."

Dustin grinned. "Do you?"

Jimmy looked at him. "I-I-I do."

"Then watch the fucking screen."

Jimmy looked upset by Dustin's use of adult language.

"Do it!" Dustin commanded. "Turn that ugly egghead of yours and watch it."

He waited until Jimmy obeyed his command, then looked inside the drawer again. As he felt around, Dustin's heart started to race with excitement.

From his peripheral, he saw Jimmy watching. Dustin approached the light switch and flipped it. Outside of the TV's glow, darkness filled the room. The lone source shined on Dustin, the eerie light molding around his body, projecting a massive, misshapen shadow over the wall behind him.

"I can see how bad you want to play," Dustin whispered, returning to the side of his bed. "And I want to play too."

Jimmy's eyes twinkled with terror. "W-what . . . what are you doing?"

Bending over, Dustin reached back into the nightstand, wrapping his fingers around the black garbage bag. When he lifted it up, the shadow on the wall behind him grew in stature. The tall silhouette dwarfed both the boys.

Dustin felt the grin on his face sharpening as he whispered, "Something you'll *never* forget."

SLEEP OVER

The nightmares were nothing new—Liv had been dealing with them for many years. Some were more intense than others, but they were always looming. It wasn't irregular for her to be awoken by one, but it wasn't the nightmare that woke her—it was the screaming.

Things had been going nicely. *Too* nicely, considering what she'd grown accustomed to expecting. Rightfully the worrywart, Liv had spent the first several hours waiting for things to go to hell. After carefully watching the two boys over dinner, she relaxed on the couch and quietly watched TV. But she wasn't just watching a program—she was on edge, waiting for some kind of disturbance to erupt.

Dustin's room was right above her, but she didn't hear a peep. For once, the house was so calm that Liv didn't even notice when she dozed off until Jimmy Stevens's screams made their way to the bottom of the stairs.

Liv's body tensed up like the sofa was on fire before shaking off the terror and shooting up from the couch as the blood-curdling cries continued.

Running through the darkness, Liv found the boy at the bottom of the stairs, tears tracing down his cheeks, chunky vomit caking his lips and shirt.

"T-t-take me h-h-home!" Jimmy shrieked.

"What hap—Is something wrong?" Liv cried, still trying to get her bearings. "What happened to you?"

The look of absolute panic in the boy's eyes shook her to the core.

"T-t-take me home! Take me h-home, n-n-now!"

"Okay, I . . . I will."

Liv didn't know what else to tell him. She couldn't deny his request—he was far too adamant.

"What the fuck is going on?" Bruce asked.

Liv looked up from the boy's glossy stare, only to find another. Bruce's bloodshot eyes were glazed over. The mixture of confusion and fear that gripped her husband wasn't common. Usually, he was angry and argumentative or stone-cold quiet when such incidents occurred. But when the smell of weed drifted through the doorway, it helped her make sense of Bruce's reaction.

"I don't know, he just—he wants to go home," Liv said, looking closer at the vomit on Jimmy's shirt. She snagged several paper towels from the kitchen and tried to clean some of the mess off the boy. "Might be sick or something."

Bruce scratched the side of his face nervously. "Sick? Sick from what?"

"T-take me hooooooome!" Jimmy wailed.

"I—I am, sweetie," Liv replied, scooping up more of the chunks and looking back at Bruce. "I said I don't know!"

The stress of the situation was starting to make her react with a bit of her own outrage.

"I do . . ." Bruce said, glaring up the dark stairwell. "There's only one virus inside this goddamn house."

Liv finished wiping Jimmy off and approached Bruce. She made sure to get close enough so he was the only one who could hear her.

"Don't jump to conclusions," Liv whispered.

"I knew it was too fucking good to be true," Bruce whispered, still looking up the staircase with a twinkle of hatred in his eyes. "I knew it."

She noticed that he was trying to suppress a tremble that seemed to rock his entire body. She'd never seen him rattled in such a way.

"Honey, look at me." Liv used her clean hand and forced his eyes to connect with hers. "You picked a shitty night to get high. I need you to focus."

"Pleeeeeeaaaase, t-t-t-take me home," Jimmy cried again.

Liv looked back at the boy. "I will!" Taking another deep breath, she reeled herself in. "Sorry, I didn't mean to snap at you. Just relax, though . . . We're leaving. Right now." She turned back to Bruce. "I have to drop him off. I need you to find out what Dustin's done. Keep your cool and hold it together, but find out what happened. And . . . make sure he's okay . . ."

Bruce's face transitioned to a ghostly pale complexion.

"What?" she asked.

As he shook his head, Liv didn't believe it was the drugs that forced the words out of Bruce's mouth. It was most likely the many years of trauma he looked to be reliving. Bruce's eyes shifted to the puke clinging to Jimmy's chin, then back to Liv.

"He'll *never* be okay."

FEAR OF THE UNKNOWN

The last thing Bruce wanted to do was investigate. Right after the door slammed shut and Liv sped down the long driveway with Jimmy, the terror truly took hold of him. The fear of the unknown paired with the voice in his head that was jabbering on uncontrollably. It didn't even feel like the thoughts were coming from his own brain.

What the fuck did Dustin do to that kid? Would he try and do something to me?!

He'd never known Dustin to be violent. He said awful things, made threats, talked back, and had an extremely perverted mind, but never resorted to violence. Bruce's gut instinct seemed to suggest that maybe this night was different.

The vomit . . . what the fuck made him vomit?

Before any of his questions could be answered, Bruce knew he'd need to confront Dustin. The combination of drugs in his system made the walls and the darkness feel alive. He was no longer enjoying the abstract movement and unsettling blurriness like he had when he was locked in the safe confines of his office.

Just relax. Turn on the lights.

But he couldn't relax. He could feel his breathing getting more labored. Reaching for the switch, Bruce activated the lights near the stairwell.

Spud stood in the doorway of the office, a low whimper escaping his tiny mouth. For a moment, Bruce hoped the dog might accompany him upstairs, but that idea was quickly dismissed when Spud darted into the living room and hid behind the couch.

"Damn," he mumbled, refocusing back on the stairs in front of him. "Dustin?" Bruce cautiously took the first step. As he continued to ascend, he repeated his son's name but got no response.

Once he reached the second floor, Bruce hit the next light switch, illuminating the landing and hallway. Staring ahead, he passed his and Liv's bedroom and the upstairs bathroom, keying in on the door at the end of the hallway, cracked open.

"Whatever you've done, we can figure it out." Inching up to the bedroom door and wrapping his fingers around the knob, Bruce found himself hesitating. An unnerving anxiety paralyzed his body. "There's no need to worry, okay?"

Bruce could hear the violent thudding of his heart in his ears as they grew hot. In no way did he want to find out what was on the other side of that door, but the voice inside drove him forward.

Open it. You've got to open it.

As the door swung open, darkness confronted him. He saw no one in the room, only the dim glow of the television screen. Turning on the light, Bruce immediately saw a puddle of vomit on the rug beside the chair. The cocktail of meds and drugs swirling inside him made the chunks look like they were alive and squirming.

Terror overcame him, and he started to feel the moisture from his sweat beading down the sides of his face. Quickly, he checked Dustin's closet and underneath his bed. His heart somehow raced even faster as he realized his son was nowhere to be found.

But a glimmer on the side of Dustin's bed caught Bruce's eye. Suddenly feeling that time was of the essence, he raced toward it.

As he rounded the corner of the mattress, he slowed in front of the shiny plastic. Bending over, Bruce picked up the item. The lack of resistance indicated that the garbage bag he held was empty.

"What the fuck?" Bruce whispered.

The lights and TV abruptly cut out.

You've gotta be kidding me.

The horrible feeling swirling around in Bruce's guts turned sour, creating a stabbing pain that he could only identify as instinct. There was a battle in his mind over what he should be more concerned about: the absence of his son or what the boy might be capable of.

I've gotta find him.

As Bruce rushed back out the door, he noticed an over-sized shadow projected in the hallway. The moonlight bleeding in through the hallway windows painted a sinister outline across the wall, warping it to look like an insidious smear of darkness that was alive and unwell. It was only after following the legs of the figure that Bruce realized it was his own shadow.

Trying to push the thought of the unsettling outline from his mind, he dashed down the hallway and staircase. It was only when he was back on the first floor and facing the door to his office that he recalled that he hadn't closed it. There was only one person who could have.

"Dustin?!"

Opening the door, he found the room empty. The window behind his recliner remained open, a soft breeze toying with the remnants of smoke still slithering up from the ashtray. Backing out of the office, Bruce tried the light switch downstairs.

Nothing.

Couldn't have blown a fuse . . . there's no storm, and the wiring is practically new.

Eyeing the door to the basement, Bruce first retreated to the kitchen, looking under the sink. Various supplies were sat stacked on a small shelf, including a flashlight.

Clicking on the flashlight, Bruce used its beam to slice through the rest of the kitchen and living room. Finding no trace of Dustin, he approached the basement door and took a deep breath.

Just go.

Bruce pulled the door open and trudged down the stairs. Each step he took brought him closer to quelling his curiosity, but he still wasn't sure if he was prepared to face reality. When his feet contacted the cold stone floor, Bruce was going to aim the light directly at the breaker box. But before he could key in on it, something stopped him dead in his tracks.

The flashlight fell upon the teeth that made up Dustin's uneven grin. The shadow on the rough cement wall beyond him didn't mimic his anatomy and seemed to be dancing. Bruce did his best to steady the beam, but the worrying silhouette still moved.

"What . . . what's—?"

Bruce's words were cut off at the sound of a switch activating in the corner of the cellar. The hanging bulb just a few feet from Dustin filled with light as Bruce turned his attention to the breaker box.

The small gray door was ajar, and he could plainly see the primary lever that controlled the entire house was switched to the ON position. Maybe the most unnerving aspect of the situation was the moment Bruce realized that a fourteen-year-old boy wouldn't understand such things—especially one as disinterested with learning as Dustin.

"What the hell . . .?" Bruce whispered.

Dustin's eyes slowly widened but stayed glued to his father. Something Bruce had said seemed to make the boy's ears perk up.

"If all the people who spoke so freely about Hell actually had the chance to get a glimpse of it, then I think they'd choose their words more carefully."

Still stupefied by the series of events, Bruce struggled to find the right thing to say in response. But with the room now lit and his attention fixed on Dustin, something else had been revealed: a length of old rope, strung over the wooden beam, swaying beside a flipped-over bucket.

Out of nowhere, it hit Bruce like a cinderblock to the gut. All the anger, anxiety, and frustration pent up inside him dissolved. Overwhelmed by guilt, all the awful and sometimes harsh things he'd thought about Dustin started to circulate in his head. He fell to his knees, expelling an inhuman howl, hysterically sucking air in and out.

He'd blamed Dustin for many things over the years, and even daydreamed about a life without him. But seeing his boy grinning beside that bucket and rope broke him. Despite all the twisted dimensions of Dustin's personality that Bruce had seen, in that moment he only saw the one he loved. The sweet boy who, years ago, used to laugh at his jokes and thought the world of his father. To imagine that boy hanging from a rope and never speaking to him again was his darkest moment. Weeping uncontrollably, Bruce clawed at his hair.

"I-I'm sorry, Son," he cried. "I just want you to be okay. I . . . I just want you to be happy."

Bruce lifted his head and noticed a blackness hovering around Dustin's eyes.

"I think happiness is just two completely different things for us," Dustin said, caressing the rope. "I wish you'd try *my* happiness. If you did, then you'd see that things could be different."

COMPETING QUESTIONS

Liv stepped out of the shower, drying herself off. It felt good considering she hadn't had one in two days. They'd returned home so late from the hospital that she'd hardly gotten any sleep. She'd hoped that a little cold water, in conjunction with several cups of coffee, could wake her up enough to fuel her through the day.

Dustin only spent one night at the hospital before they released him, and Liv stayed with him. He'd been there several times before for various incidents, and she'd watched him during his visits—he knew exactly what to say to the doctors to put them at ease and put himself on a path to rapid release. He always somehow had all the answers they wanted.

Part of her hoped that something good would come out of the incident, that it might somehow bring them closer together. The raw emotion she'd seen in Bruce when he explained to her what happened—and, more importantly, how it impacted him—could be a turning point toward resetting their family. But it must've been the drugs that brought such emotions out of Bruce because he was cold as ever just hours afterward.

She was so wound up about everything, she didn't even have time to process her own emotions yet.

Bruce's description of what happened had shaken her. Dustin had spoken of taking his own life and the lives of others before, but it had always turned out to be nothing but nasty comments. There was never any evidence that he was actually going to hurt himself or someone else.

Is this *the turning point?* Liv thought. *Is he getting worse?*

Not only had she not digested what happened to her son, but she hadn't even considered the other boy. The guilt brought on by her thought made Liv recall her drive with Jimmy Stevens. The horrible sounds replayed over and over again. The quiet squealing, muffled by Jimmy's closed lips, had lasted for the duration of the car ride. Just looking at him, Liv could tell that he'd clearly experienced some severe trauma. The terror and torment that he was dealing with were as unsettling as they were heartbreaking. Liv had tried to comfort him some, but the boy just kept his mouth shut.

Upon seeing his son, Jimmy's father, Russell, had been furious. He'd demanded an explanation as to why his son was so upset. Unfortunately, Liv didn't have an answer— she *still* didn't have an answer. The only people who knew what happened were Dustin and Jimmy.

After accusing her of negligence and threatening to call the police, Russell had eventually shifted his emotions. Transitioning from angry to concerned, he'd told her to leave and turned his focus to calming his son.

Russell was such a kind man on the phone, she hadn't imagined him capable of such rage. But Liv understood. When it came to their child, parents were unpredictable.

Oh, God, the school! Would Russell say something to them?

With everything going relatively smoothly at the Carter School, the idea that an outside factor might ruin it all gave Liv a dreadful feeling.

She took a deep breath and looked back into the shower. A clump of her fiery hair sat in the drain. Grimacing, she felt at her locks.

Don't cry. If you start now, you won't stop. Just get to work.

She didn't know if the stress of life was responsible for her increasing hair loss or if it was genetic. Her mother had died before she ever had a chance to bring it up.

Mom . . .

Flashes of that night at the house erupted in her mind. The horrifying grimace on her mother's face when Liv and Bruce had found her in the basement that morning was an image that would never leave her. Of course, dying—for anyone—would be the scariest thing to face. But there was something about her expression that still haunted Liv . . . almost as if something happened to her mother that was beyond her comprehension.

The medical examiner found nothing strange about the death. Alice had heart issues that she took medication for and died of a massive stroke. But no one was ever able to come up with a plausible explanation as to why it would've happened in the basement.

What reason would she even have to be down there?

The part that really stuck with her—outside of her mother's death—was what had happened afterward. When Liv returned from the basement, despite how much she was shrieking and crying, Dustin remained seated on the couch. With his gawk of blankness staring Liv in the face, her son said nothing. There was no trying to comfort her, there was no concern, not even a hint of nosiness. It was like the curious little boy who always had questions about even the most mundane affairs was suddenly dead.

Why didn't he even ask what happened?

Part of her initially believed that, despite finding him upstairs, maybe he'd seen what happened.

Was it Mom's death that was the turning point?

Liv had been grieving so deeply after her mother passed that it was hard to remember now. She'd grown up fatherless, and outside of her mother, she had no other family. Bruce had been amazing—he waited on her hand and foot and dealt with her mood swings and allowed her to vent. But maybe he had been too focused on her while she was too focused on herself.

Did we forget about Dustin?

She shuddered, trying to push the thoughts of her mother's ghastly frown out of her mind. Reaching down, Liv plucked the wad of hair from the drain, hiding it in a few sheets of toilet paper before stuffing it into the trash. The hair loss embarrassed her deeply and made her feel even uglier. The last thing she wanted was for Bruce to have *another* reason to be put off by her. She hoped to hide it from him as long as possible—or at least until they could find a way to rekindle their flame.

When she dropped the paper into the bin, the black bag caught her eye. The only information Bruce had been able to relay to her the prior night was that he'd found a black garbage bag inside Dustin's room. He knew nothing about what the bag was used for or what had transpired between Jimmy and Dustin.

As Liv wrapped the towel around her body and returned to her bedroom, the question tortured her.

What could he have done to Jimmy?

When she opened her underwear drawer, what she saw lying inside answered that question. One of the several sex toys she'd tried to rid herself of days prior sat atop her underwear. The chunks and liquid elements of the vomit had dried and hardened, bonding the sticky shaft of the dildo to the pair of panties.

ACTING NORMAL

Liv carefully watched her coworkers seated at the desks around her. When the coast was clear, she slipped another pill inside her mouth and then discreetly washed it down with her coffee. Just knowing the drugs were en route helped.

Just act normal, she thought, trying her best to keep everything bottled. *Nobody knows . . .*

There was one thing besides taking the pills she did at work that always helped dull the pain. A distraction that occupied her brain and kept her from thinking too much about things at home.

She slid the bottom drawer of her desk open to reveal her stash. Chips, cheese puffs, beef jerky, candy, and more stared back at her. Her stomach rumbled with excitement but not out of hunger.

Bending down, obscured by her desk, she started to shovel loads of the snacks into her mouth. She wasn't really focused on exactly what she was eating, just that she *was* eating. As she chewed a piece of jerky, a mouthful of corn chips, and several gummy bears all at once, a strange feeling of relief came over her—a wave of cheap distraction.

While Liv's brain tried to diagnose the variety of flavors on her palate, she forgot about the fear. And as her jaw motion mashed the contents of her mouth, she forgot about the hurt.

"Hey, Liv," came a man's voice.

Trying to quickly sit back up, Liv smacked her head against the underside of her desk. The jarring collision caused her to bite down on her tongue.

When she rose up, she realized it was Fredson Dennard again—the man who sat a few seats over. Liv tried to finish chewing so she could talk. The iron taste of her blood meshed with the other sweet and salty flavors, tainting her snacking experience. She finally swallowed and forced a smile.

"H-hey! What's up?"

Fred's face was wrinkled with concern. "Is . . . is that blood on your teeth?"

"Oh, yeah—sorry, I-I just, ah, accidentally bit my tongue."

"Ouch. Looks like it hurts."

Liv shrugged. "I'll be okay. I'm always okay."

"Well . . . I don't really know how to say this . . ." He bit his lip for a moment.

Dread inflated Liv's stomach as the fear returned. Fear of the unknown, tormenting her.

"I'm just . . . I'm worried about you, Liv," Fred said, concern glimmering in his eyes.

Liv was taken aback by the statement. "What makes you think something's wrong?"

Fred rolled her eyes. "Listen, we might not be best friends, but we've worked together in this office for a while now. We talk often enough that I think you can probably tell that I care about you."

"Fred, I appreciate it, but really, I'm fi—"

"There's no reason to lie. I've heard you crying in the supply closet. Several times."

Liv didn't protest his assertion.

"I like to think I'm a pretty good judge of character. For example, I knew you were a total sweetheart from the moment I met you. You were someone I wanted to be around because you have this kind and . . . loving aura. You care about others . . . just like I do."

It was hard for Liv to deny that what Fred was telling her felt good to hear. During the countless times they'd chatted, Liv had always just imagined that he was being polite—conversing out of courtesy rather than desire. After all, Fred was a handsome and fit man who could've probably had his pick of the women in the office. But he always seemed to want to strike up a conversation with her. It made Liv feel special—special in ways she hadn't felt in a long time.

Fred sighed. "You know, I only met Bruce that one time at the office Christmas party, but I could tell right away that he didn't appreciate you. He just doesn't understand how lucky he is to have someone like you. Most men don't." Fred leaned over and put his hand on Liv's. "And do you wanna know why?"

The words made Liv's nose sting. She was already an emotional mess long before their talk started, and she was doing everything in her power to keep herself from breaking down. Considering all the pressure she'd been dealing with because of Bruce and Dustin, she was barely hanging on.

Liv didn't want to ask Fred why—she didn't know where that would potentially drive the conversation. But after everything he'd said, she felt obligated to. The conversation was starting to wear on her. All the stress was bubbling up inside. The tension from the situation with Dustin was horrible, but somehow, it wasn't the worst thing.

Not being wanted, and having to share a bed with the very person who didn't want her, was the worst thing.

"Why?" Liv finally asked.

"Because most men are self-absorbed assholes," Fred replied. "Coldhearted and thickheaded."

The intensity that was transmitted as his deep gaze beamed down like two spotlights made Liv feel like she was about to melt. Her body felt like it was being prodded with countless pins and needles.

"So . . . I came over here today to tell you that I'm *not* one of them," Fred said. "And I just wanted you to know that I appreciate you. Always have. You're an incredible person, and I think you haven't heard that enough."

Covering her mouth with her free hand, Liv hid her quivering lip. She tried to brush it off and forced herself to pull it together again.

"And if you ever need someone to talk to, I'm here," Fred said. "It's as simple as that, okay?"

Over the years, Liv had learned to mask her misery so well with a cheerful tone. But clearly, her body language and the closet breakdowns had given her away. She shook her head, but as her faux smile started to dissipate, the motion turned into a nod.

"Thank you," Liv whispered. "That . . . that means a lot. I've always enjoyed our chats."

Fred kept his hand rested on hers longer than she expected, gently rubbing it with his thumb. It was like he didn't want to let go.

"I'm glad. I've been wanting to tell you this for a while now, but I never had the courage. But hearing you in the closet earlier, I knew I had to." He cleared his throat. "And just know this . . . you're better than whatever it is that's trying to hold you down."

A strange tingle buzzed around inside her. They'd been friends for a long time, but as of late, Liv had grown more introverted than maybe she even realized. But there was something about the way Fred caressed her hand that seemed different than any other time they'd spent together. The feeling might've been even more intense to Liv due to the lack of sincere care and attention in her life. The absence of affection was making her think crazy.

With his free hand, Fred snagged a pen from the cup and scribbled his phone number on Liv's desk calendar. "Call me anytime you need . . . or want me."

Liv felt hotness on her cheeks.

Is . . . is he coming on to me?

She wasn't sure exactly what he'd meant before. He could've just been trying to be nice out of pity, but as she looked down at the phone number, she felt otherwise. She locked eyes with him. The warmth spread from her head to the rest of her body. Flustered by their interaction, Liv knew her face must've been turning red.

Brrriiinnggg!

The phone on Liv's desk interrupted the intense stare they were tangled in.

"I . . . I should get that," she said.

"You should," Fred replied. He slowly pried his fingers off hers and pulled his hand back, but it looked like it pained him to do so. "But don't forget about what I said."

Brrriiinnggg!

Liv nodded and smiled, watching Fred slowly walk away. His toned backside and snug physique were hard not to admire. There was something about the way he'd made her feel that was almost like the drugs she took, but better.

Liv was so starved for love that she didn't realize her cell phone was already in her hand taking a picture of Fred's number.

Brrriiinnggg!

As she slipped her cell back into her purse, she lifted the phone and put it against her ear.

"Bookkeeping Solutions, this is Liv speak—"

"I'm on my way to pick you up," Bruce said. "We need to go to Dustin's school. Right now."

The odd moment of sweetness and bliss instantly evaporated—she was back in the nightmare. Liv could suddenly hear the thunderous beating of her pulse inside her hot ears.

"W-why?" she asked, shaking her head. "What's going on? Did something happen?"

Bruce paused, sighing. She could hear the distress in his voice. "He tried to light the fucking school on fire."

UP IN FLAMES

"I have no choice but to expel him," Justine said. Her eyes were like bayonets staring across her desk.

Liv wasn't shocked by her statement, nor did Bruce seem to be. But that didn't stop the instant shot of dread from being unleashed inside her. She was already on the verge of a heart attack when Bruce had made her aware of the situation, but the good news was that no one had been hurt. Still, if Dustin was expelled from the Carter School, that was going to create an entirely new set of problems.

"But—but how do you know someone else didn't bring the lighter?" Bruce asked.

Justine smiled, but in an annoyed way. Reaching into the drawer beside her, she retrieved a shiny object. She set the lighter down in front of them—a vintage, custom Zippo with the letters *B.H.* etched into it.

"Because your initials are engraved in it."

Liv saw the same tired look overcome Bruce. They'd been through this routine many times before, but it wasn't getting any easier.

"Oh, c'mon," he said, slapping his hand against his thigh with frustration. Despite staring defeat in the face, he still wasn't willing to admit to it.

Justine straightened up. She seemed ready for a fight if necessary. "What? You're saying it's *not* yours?"

There was a beat of silence before Bruce picked up the lighter and slipped it inside his pocket.

Ironically, the old lighter was a wedding gift from Liv that Bruce had used to light his celebratory cigar after their ceremony. With Bruce so deep in the antique business, she figured it would be a great choice. Liv hadn't seen the lighter in such a long time that she was surprised the thing still worked.

He must've dusted it off to smoke his weed.

Justine sucked her teeth, exuding irritation. "We can deal with a child that has issues—that's why we're here—but what we can't deal with is oblivious parenting. With a history like Dustin's, this could've and *should've* been prevented—"

"You're—you're right," Liv interrupted gently. "We definitely screwed up. But please, Justine, I'm begging you to reconsider. Dustin . . . he was doing so good here."

"I thought so too," Justine said. "Until I received a phone call early this morning that made me think otherwise. I spoke with a very concerned and angry parent. One who says Dustin assaulted his son during a sleepover at *your* house."

Liv stayed quiet while Bruce hung his head.

"Now, it would be one thing if this lighter situation was the only issue, but there are other accusations. Accusations that I'm afraid make keeping your son here a liability."

"Please," Liv begged, "we'll check him every day—make sure he never leaves the house with anything like that ever again. And—and no more students over at our house."

"I'm afraid the situation is too . . . dire for promises," Justine replied. "My heart aches for you, it truly does. I may sound a bit curt in this moment, but that's only due to the seriousness of this situation." She glanced out the window and scratched her chin. "I took this job specifically to help boys like Dustin and parents like you."

Bruce gritted his teeth, the discussion clearly not going the way he'd hoped.

Justine pulled some paperwork closer. "But I can't do so at the risk of everyone else in my care. If the sprinkler system had malfunctioned, one flaming curtain could've turned into a building of burning children, and we might not be having this conversation."

"We'll pay you double," Bruce said.

Justine shook her head and pushed the papers toward them. "I'm not sure how else I can say it. As of today, we've terminated the automatic billing, but the Carter School's legal team is in the process of evaluating the total damage estimate. I imagine they'll be following up with you in the near future." The principal gestured to a woman standing just outside the door. "Shauna has all of Dustin's belongings bagged up. She'll provide them to you before bringing you to your son."

Liv pulled the paperwork close to her chest, trying to contain the anxiety and sadness swelling inside her.

"I really do wish you both—I mean, the three of you—the very best," Justine said.

Bruce and Liv both rose from their chairs.

Liv felt the hotness of embarrassment on her face and the rumble of terror in her gut. It was like being fired, only worse. When you got fired, normally you could just apply for a new job. But that wasn't the case here. They were at the mercy of a care network that had run out of patience. She had no idea how long it might take for her to get Dustin placed in another school.

Bruce turned to the door before pausing and pivoting back toward Justine. The desperation Liv noticed in his eyes was uncomfortable to look at, and she could tell the principal wanted nothing more than to forget she'd ever met them. For someone in her position, it was probably the key to staying sane.

"There's got to be somewhere else you can refer us to . . . somewhere new, maybe?" he begged. "Please . . ."

Justine sighed. "I'm afraid these institutions don't just pop up overnight."

"So, what, am I supposed to just quit my fucking job and stay home with him?!" Spittle flew from Bruce's lips.

"Mr. Huxley, considering everything that's transpired today, taking that type of tone with me after *your* oversight put *my* life, and the lives of the staff and children, in danger doesn't seem fair nor logical. I don't have to say another word to you and I don't think I will. Now get out of my office. Right away."

Her argument was undeniable. Bruce turned to the door and whipped it against the wall, too agitated to hold it for his wife.

Liv was having a full-on breakdown as she turned toward the exit. But before she could take another step, the principal's voice grabbed her attention.

"Hey, Liv," she said.

Liv remained static with her back to her. She was still but clearly listening—so desperate for direction that she had no choice.

"It's nothing personal," Justine said. "I always liked and admired your effort. And I hope you understand that I just can't tolerate the type of attitude your husband has after such a . . . frightening day."

Liv sniffed the runny snot back up her nose. "It's no problem. I . . . I understand."

"Here, have a tissue," Justine said, lifting the box on her desk forward.

"I-I'm okay," Liv lied.

"All right."

"I'm sorry." She wiped a tear from her eye. "I really wish things hadn't gone this way."

Justine nodded. "I know you are. And so am I. But listen . . . I know you're probably already wondering what's next for Dustin and trying to figure out how to find him care without losing your jobs. I imagine it's quite stressful. And while there isn't an overnight solution, I do have a suggestion that may be able to aid you in your search."

Liv turned to face her. "Really?"

"It's the age of the internet, and we're really lucky that's the case."

"Okay, I'm listening."

"There are some other, less *conventional* options outside of traditional schools and clinics. Behavioral therapists that might be able to come to you and keep things steady while you continue to search for a permanent solution. It could be expensive though—"

"Money's not an issue."

"Okay." Justine smiled. "That's good. Then I would strongly recommend a website called The Rolodex."

A speck of hope suddenly swirled in Liv's quaking stomach. She nodded. "Thank you . . . this means the world. What is the site for, exactly?"

"Well, it's a search engine of sorts. It takes key words entered by the user, based on the intended patient's symptoms, and suggests qualified, independent therapists and medical personnel with complementary expertise. It's relatively new, but quite advanced, from what I'm told."

Liv stretched out her shaky arm, accepting the olive branch as they shook hands. Her voice quivered when she spoke. "Thank you. You have no idea how much I needed this."

Justine nodded. "Actually, I think I do."

After a few shakes Liv turned back to the door. But before she could exit the room, the principal interrupted once more.

"Just know that it's best to be up front with them," she said. "It'll be a tough sell, but with a little luck, I bet you'll find someone willing to help."

With wet eyes, Liv focused on the new set of problems circulating in her mind. She felt overwhelmed by the sudden shift and dangerous nature of what was supposed to be a normal day. There was nothing else she could do but take the advice and pray that things got better.

"Okay," Liv said. "I'll be sure to remember that."

THE TALK

The car ride home was silent aside from Liv's occasional sniffles. Bruce had been watching her closely. She'd dotted her nose several times with a napkin, trying to soak up the runny trail.

She couldn't talk.

She couldn't move.

She was devastated.

Bruce wasn't in the mood to talk either, but he had a different reason for holding his tongue. With his jaw clenched tight, he knew if he opened his mouth, it would be the precursor to a volcanic flood of obscenities. It'd finally happened. He'd reached the breaking point. He was doing his best to carefully choose his words, practicing what he might say in his head.

As the car pulled into their long, secluded driveway, Bruce watched Dustin fidget in his seat. His fiery red hair popped in the rearview; his hair was just like his mother's. Hardly able to look at the freckled grin on his son's face, Bruce hit the brakes angrily and threw the car into park. When he got out of the vehicle, he didn't wait for anyone. It felt like steam was hissing out of his ears—he wanted to separate himself from both of them.

But when Bruce reached the front steps, he paused, remembering that Dustin was about to get a talking-to. Not just any talking-to—the talking-to of his fucking life.

Bruce inserted the key into the door and waited for Liv and Dustin to reach the steps before opening it.

Spud roared, unleashing a barrage of enthusiastic barks. The little dachshund's brown backside wagged excitedly as Bruce and Liv entered, but the welcome party screeched to a halt when Dustin stepped inside. A muffled growl left the dog's long snout as he quickly turned his back and retreated upstairs.

Dustin was about to follow the dog when Bruce's voice boomed. "Where the hell do you think you're going?!"

Bruce watched as the boy froze in place and pivoted back to him. His fourteen-year-old face looked so innocent at times, but along with that innocence, a strange weight loomed in his eyes.

Something beyond his years.

Something dark and mysterious.

Something that—while Bruce didn't like to admit it—frightened him. But Bruce was tired of being afraid. As much as he was trying to control his emotions, he was too enraged to think straight.

Liv watched the two of them as Dustin grinned.

Something about his happiness made Bruce deeply uncomfortable, yet he couldn't pull his eyes away.

"I was gonna go to my room and draw," Dustin said.

Bruce reached over and pulled the bag that had been packed for Dustin from Liv's clutches. As he looked through his son's possessions, the fury boiled inside him. His fingers finally found what he'd been searching for. Bruce threw the notebook directly at Dustin's face. There was a carelessness to Bruce's anger that was so intense it even scared him.

"Why?!" Bruce screamed. "So you can draw more of this evil shit?!"

"Bruce!" Liv yelled.

"A fucking woman being hanged, playing with her bloody cunt?!" Bruce persisted.

The spine of the notebook was thick enough that when it smacked into Dustin's face, it left a red line over his cheek and nose. The boy didn't flinch.

When the notepad crashed onto the floor, it opened, displaying a childish sketch of a boy. And on the wall, across from the boy, stood his oversized shadow, holding a big knife. Some color had been added to highlight the crimson drips on the blade the wicked figure was holding.

"Please, stop," Liv begged. "Maybe we'd just better talk about this tomorrow instead—"

"No!" Bruce barked, pitching the bag onto the floor. "I'm done waiting for tomorrow! It's always tomorrow! Things are gonna change, and they're gonna change now!"

Liv trembled as the bag smacked against the hardwood floor. It wasn't the first time that Bruce had uncorked his temper, but it didn't happen often, and never with such an overflow of venom. It was like the dam holding his darkest rage at bay had suddenly burst.

Bruce got down on one knee in front of Dustin and grabbed him by the cheeks, squishing his lips together.

"Don't hurt him," Liv whispered, taking a step toward them. "You know he can't . . . he can't help it."

Turning back, Bruce pointed his finger at her. "Don't move another goddamn inch!"

Liv obeyed his command as the tears continued to run down her face.

He returned his focus to Dustin, his eyes burning a hole through the boy. "No more fires. No more saying nasty things. No more stealing. No more sick fucking drawings. No nothing!"

Through his smushed lips, Dustin said, "But I didn't start the fire."

Bruce loosened his grip, wondering if there was some kind of misunderstanding. His arm fell to his side. "Well, who started it, then?"

The grin that made the entire family uneasy returned to Dustin's face. "I don't know."

Grabbing him by the throat and torso, Bruce lifted the boy off the floor and stormed into the living room.

"Enough!" Bruce yelled, his eyes feeling ready to pop out of his skull.

"W-what are you doing?!" Liv shrieked.

"I've had enough of this shit!" Bruce yelled. "It ends today! He needs to understand that, in life, there's fucking consequences!"

Tossing Dustin onto the couch, Bruce unbuckled his belt and slipped it off.

Liv's eyes filled with fright. She looked like she wanted to stop him, but Bruce imagined that there was a part of her that was grateful it was just a whipping—that maybe even agreed with the punishment. That was probably the case, he told himself.

Until it started to actually happen.

"Who started the fire?!" Bruce yelled. "Who?!"

He pulled Dustin's pants down with ease. The boy didn't respond or fight him. Not when his bare ass was exposed, nor when his father gritted his teeth and raised the stiff leather above his head.

Liv shuddered as each smack connected with her son's backside, watching the effected strips of flesh grow closer to her hair color. The welts began to form, and as two lashings turned into twelve, Bruce noticed one thing remained just as consistent as his strikes: the maniacally wide grin on Dustin's face as he cooed with delight.

LATE-NIGHT REFLECTIONS

Bruce's hands trembled uncontrollably. But it wasn't *just* his hands—his entire body intermittently rattled. In the blanket of darkness surrounding him, he took some comfort. From the chair he sat in, his reflection in the mirror on the wall was obscured.

That was for the best. He couldn't bear to look himself in the eye. After such an epic meltdown, he knew with certainty the entire family would look at him differently. There was an unavoidable measure of disgust in his heart when he thought of his circumstance.

Family? he thought. *This isn't a family.* He shook his head. *What even are we?*

Despite his anger and a nagging desire to dissociate from this warped version of the American dream he was stuck in, he still felt ashamed. Bruce still wanted his family to love him—he yearned for it. He wanted to believe there was a path to unfuck their twisted situation. But now he had to ask himself another hard question: How much further away from a status quo had his violent tantrum dragged them?

I just wanna be normal. Just the basics. Please, God. I can't fucking do this for the rest of my life.

He hated talking to God. Nothing ever came of it, and this evening was no different.

He dug his nails into the chair, attempting to persuade himself that what he'd done could actually be for the best.

Maybe a good whipping was what he needed . . .

Bruce had gotten quite a few himself when he was younger. Looking back on it, he wasn't sure if it helped him or screwed him up more. But he tried to convince himself it was the former.

Sometimes, you need a good kick in the ass. People'll just destroy the entire goddamn world otherwise . . .

Sure, times had changed and the incident that just occurred could've gotten Dustin taken from them, but what other choice did he have?

Take him, please. Fucking take him, I'm begging you.

The notion didn't frighten him anywhere near as much as it excited him.

As Bruce continued to play with the fantastical thought, in the corner of his eye, he saw a black outline. In the doorway, a shadowy figure appeared without warning—silent as a cemetery at midnight and just as eerie.

When Bruce's head snapped to confront the silhouette, relief quickly washed over him. The familiar shape of disappointment: Liv's husky figure. The baby weight that never melted away. He always figured an athletic-type—like his wife—would easily work it off. He was wrong.

Fucker took that from me too.

It wasn't the first time he'd considered his son to be the root cause of his erectile dysfunction. He couldn't recall the last time he'd felt the urge to just rail his spouse like the good ol' days. Things were so different now.

"That can never happen again," Liv said, finally breaking the uncomfortable silence. She stepped a few paces closer to him, the glow of the moonlight illuminating half of her face. Her eyes looked wet and puffy.

"I know," Bruce replied.

"I mean it. I'm not fucking around."

"What would you have had me do?"

"I don't know. Not that."

Bruce's nails clamped down on the recliner even tighter. "For Christ's sake, he—he could've *killed* someone, Liv!"

"Keep your voice down!"

Bruce took a deep breath and closed his eyes. It helped settle him down.

"He finally just got to sleep," Liv said.

Bruce paused, considering his question. "How was he?" He asked it with a hint of reluctance tilting his tone.

Liv turned to the window and looked out. Trying to do normal, nonchalant things comforted her. Bruce imagined it took her mind off the madness. "He's fine. I mean, he's not *fine*, but he's fine."

Bruce huffed in disgust. Only in their house could such a contradictory remark make sense.

"It's like . . . it didn't even faze him," she whispered.

"He's ruining our lives."

"It's not just about us. He's hurting too."

"Obviously—I know that—but what the hell are we gonna do now? With his history, it's not like we can just hire *anyone* to watch him. He's a fucking liability."

"I know, but . . . we've gotta think of something." Liv scratched the back of her head. "Can you maybe just try working remotely for a little while?"

He sighed with extra anxiousness this time. "Remotely? I'm the manager, I can't just—"

"You just told me the other day that, like, seventy percent of the sales Carnegie's makes are online. Can't you just figure something out and be a little flexible for once? I'd do it myself, but you know I can't. I just work in an office. You're the fucking manager."

"Point taken. I suppose I can try to work something out. But if I'm here—around him—having to babysit all day, I'm not gonna be able to get any actual work done."

"You'll only have to do it for a few days. Just until I can find some kind of alternative. I'll take care of that part, I promise."

Bruce nodded. "Okay. Deal."

"Thank you."

Liv nervously picked at her finger. "I'll try to make some calls on my lunchbreak tomorrow."

"Where? That cunt in the office made it seem like we just burned our last bridge."

"Please don't call her that."

"I wouldn't call her it if she didn't act like it."

Liv rolled her eyes. "What did you expect? Dustin nearly burned down the school. She meant well. After you left, she gave me a lead."

"A lead?" Bruce asked.

"It's some kind of search engine or something. Might be able to help us find a specialist that can treat Dustin here while we're at work."

"Right."

Bruce's face displayed the *I'll believe it when I see it* look. Normally, the look would've aggravated Liv, but it was clear her mind was preoccupied with other thoughts. But Bruce was curious enough to pause and look at her. As she stood solemnly by the window, glowing in the moonlight, in a state of deep ponderance, he finally bit.

"What is it?"

Liv kept her eyes out the window, utterly lost in the nothingness. It was like she was trying to will herself to finally speak.

"Were you upstairs before?"

The question baffled him. "When?"

"While I was upstairs with Dustin."

"No . . . I haven't been upstairs since this morning. Why?"

She shook her head. "It's . . . it's nothing. Forget it."

Furrowing his brow, Bruce said, "Well, now you've *gotta* tell me."

"I . . . just . . . I thought I saw you in the hallway."

"What the fuck are you talking about?"

"I saw a shadow—a big, tall shadow at the end of the hallway."

Bruce thought back to what he'd seen in the basement that night with Dustin. Picturing the unsettling darkness slithering on the wall made him shudder. He wasn't sure if the chemical cocktail had brought to life a figment of his imagination or not, but if that was the case, he had no desire to feed into it. He allowed Liv to continue talking, purposely not sharing his experience.

"Like I said, I'm sure it was nothing," she said.

He squinted in disbelief as he studied her.

"But on a more serious note," she went on. "Can I trust that you're not going to freak out on Dustin tomorrow?"

She transitioned to the subject with ease. They'd been together long enough that Liv was relatively seamless at moving on when something got under Bruce's skin. It had served her well before, and even better in that moment.

"We'll be fine," he grumbled.

"Now *that* sounds reassuring." Liv smiled as she poured on the sarcasm. It was something they connected on—or, at least, they used to.

Bruce picked up on her quip. For the first time in several hours, he felt the tension reduce. The connection that brought them so far together was faded but still there. Even if it needed work, he took comfort in knowing that, to some extent, they were on the same side.

Adjusting his tone to a nerdy pitch, he said, "I'm glad I could instill such confidence in you."

They shared a minor chuckle.

"Ugh . . . I'm so tired," Liv said, yawning the words out. "Can we go to bed now?"

Despite the momentary high note, something about her prior remark stuck with him and didn't sit well. The "shadow" comment was so out of left field. He hoped she wasn't losing her mind. He was surprised they'd both held it together for as long as they had. They hadn't done it alone, of course—they were *both* heavily medicated. Amid the swirling, constant chaos, the pills were all they had to keep their own personal darknesses subdued.

For a split second, Bruce wondered if Dustin's mental issues could be hereditary. He recalled the stories Liv had told him about her mother, Alice, in the past. Stories that didn't paint her in the best light. He'd only interacted with Alice on a limited basis before she'd passed away, so it was hard to determine if the way Liv viewed her was accurate or not. She had always been sweet as pie around him.

He dismissed the hypothesis—Liv had never said anything so outlandish before. It was most likely Dustin's disturbing drawings and vile mumblings that implanted the erroneous suggestion into her subconscious. While Bruce couldn't be sure about much anymore, one thing was certain: he was tired of thinking.

"Well?" Liv said.

He nodded and stood up from the recliner. "I'd give my left nut for this goddamn day to be over."

EASY ON THE EYES

Her tits were ridiculous. They barely fit into her tank top, and as she bent sideways to stretch, Bruce lost himself in her cavern of cleavage. The girl was thick but athletic—just like Liv used to be.

YogaGal98—or Natalia Nuñez, as he knew her real name to be—was required viewing. He had alerts set up for when her new videos dropped. Watching her work out was his escape—an escape he found himself dipping into more frequently as of late. To Bruce, she was perfect. Everything he could've wanted and everything he didn't have.

Natalia's dark, caramel skin and dreamy eyes were the perfect complement to her voluptuous curves. Even the slightly crooked tooth on one side of her mouth somehow made her cuter in his eyes. Her exotic tone helped comfort Bruce. She instructed so calmly and caringly—it was like she was talking directly to *him*.

It was more than just a sexual thing, but it was still very much a sexual thing.

Bruce's eyes flashed up to his work laptop. There were a few emails, but nothing important. He removed his set of noise-canceling headphones from his desk and plugged them into the personal laptop sitting beside his work-issued computer.

Spud jumped up on the side of the chair, begging for attention. He had a twinkle in his eyes, like he wanted something.

"What is it, boy?" Bruce asked. "You wanna go pee-pees? You wanna go outside?"

The dog had just shit not but an hour ago, but still, Bruce knew his sweet boy was getting older and his bladder was growing weaker with each passing day.

Locking his phone, Bruce set it on the desk, then exited his office. He looked up the stairs, past the banister, to the area in front of Dustin's door. It remained closed. He hadn't heard the boy come out of his room all morning.

It was the way Bruce preferred it.

Switching his attention to the front door, he opened it halfway, then turned to Spud.

"You wanna go outside?"

The dog bypassed his offer and trotted into the kitchen instead, whimpering near his food bowl.

"Shit, I can't believe I forgot to feed you! Sorry, buddy." He reached into the cupboard for a can of dogfood and popped the top. "As you know, shit's been just a little crazy around here."

The congealed beef chunks thudded into the dish, and Bruce tossed the can into the trash.

"All right, enjoy. I'll be back in a few."

When he returned to his office, he quietly locked the door. Sliding back into his chair, Bruce promptly loaded a website called Porn Planet on his personal laptop. He typed the key words "Latina girl moans loud while getting fucked" and clicked search. Excitedly, he hit the play button on one of the videos and slipped on his headphones.

He skipped ahead through the ludicrous storyline right to the hardcore sex scene. The first girl's moans weren't exactly how *his* YogaGal98 sounded. The attire and attractiveness of the porn star didn't matter so much—he wouldn't have his eyes on them anyway.

He cycled through several other videos, searching for a voice that was as sweet and wholesome as Natalia's.

While he didn't find an exact match, he was too horny to wait any longer. Bruce quickly unzipped his pants and maneuvered his erection out of his boxers. He hadn't even loaded Natalia's video yet and precum was already dribbling from his tip. When he unlocked his smartphone, the anticipation only grew.

Escape was only a few clicks away.

LEFT TO HIS OWN DEVICES

The dog had snapped at Dustin several times before he got the T-shirt over Spud's head. With the dog unable to see, Dustin could get one of the plastic six-pack rings around its neck. Tied to the end of the six-pack rings was a makeshift rope comprised of several shoelaces.

Even before, when he'd cornered the dachshund in the kitchen, the animal's reaction showed that it knew it needed to protect itself. Every time Spud was in the same room as Dustin, he was *always* on guard. But the attempted bites hadn't prevented him from bringing the dog upstairs into the privacy of his lair.

The shoelaces were laid over the top of the bedroom door and wrapped around the handle on the other side. Spud was elevated on his hind legs—an uncomfortable pose for his older frame.

As Dustin pulled harder on the laces, the dog was elevated even higher, the unforgiving plastic from the soda can rings remaining snug around his neck, cutting off his air supply. The spasming pup shook violently, trying to wrestle free to no avail.

"That's it, boy," Dustin whispered. "Choke for me."

He looked down at the dog's dick, watching the red rocket unsheathe from the mound of skin. The presence of Spud's arousal only confirmed what Dustin already knew.

"I knew you'd like it. Let it take you there—take you to the best place. Don't be afraid . . . Enjoy it while it lasts. When you get there, I know you'll thank me."

Dustin pictured the hanging men and women from all those years ago in the basement. He saw them as clear as Spud's pecker. The image of them all toying with their genitals in unison as they choked and drooled made him feel bad for the dog. As he focused on Spud's paws, he realized that the poor little fella couldn't do that for himself.

Reaching out with his shoe, he used the toe to bat around the dog's erection. As it grew harder, the dog flailed about, triggering the makeshift noose to elevate him another inch or so.

"You're almost there, boy . . ."

The profound agony in Spud's struggle to breathe made Dustin salivate. The pain and distress that he was syphoning from the hound was everything.

Dustin enjoyed focusing on the sounds—same as he'd done when shoving his mom's dildo down Jimmy Stevens's throat. No matter who he was attempting to enlighten, hearing them choke, moan, or wail was of paramount importance. The intense pain in Spud's low cries was almost orgasmic. Listening to his claws scrape wildly against the wooden door as his tiny body tried its damnedest to squirm free was enthralling.

Of the several sex toys his mother had thrown away, Dustin had chosen the thickest one for Jimmy—the louder it sounded going in, the better. But the dog was on the verge of choking to death, and the plastic cutting off the hound's air supply was muffling the sounds he was emitting. Dustin truly wished there was some magical way to turn up the volume.

It wasn't *just* the dog's pain that made him feel better. It was knowing how much his parents—particularly Bruce—cared for the dog. Spud was the only thing in the house that seemed to make his father smile.

It would be interesting to see how he handled such a revelation. Since his parents wouldn't accept the enlightenment he constantly tried to bestow on them, it was long overdue that he create an example. Dustin found both comfort and anticipation when he considered how strangling the beloved dog would make his parents feel.

This'll show them, Dustin thought. *She'll probably just take another pill and cry. Him, though . . . he's going to lose his fucking mind.*

Dustin adjusted his arm to keep the laces tense. The constant pressure of the dog's weight was starting to wear on him. Fighting off the fatigue as best he could, Dustin bit his lip as he watched Spud's movements slow.

Most of the sunlight in Dustin's room was blocked out by the thick curtains, but just enough leaked through to make his shadow look like a mesmerizing projection on the wall. As Dustin's grip started to slip, the tall black outline on the wall reached for the shadow of the laces and offered its strength, holding it steady.

"Good puppy," Dustin growled through his wide grin. "Thatta boy."

EASY ON THE EARS

"I can't believe this is the first time we've done this," Liv said, taking a drink of her vodka spritz.

"Seriously, what the hell were we thinking?" Fred asked.

As she looked around the bar, she realized they were pretty much the only people in the place.

"Man, I haven't been to a dive bar—or even had a drink—in I can't even remember how long," she said.

She couldn't help but look into his eyes. They felt like a place of comfort and safety. Somewhere she could get lost in if she wasn't careful.

"I've probably been coming to these places a little too much," Fred replied.

"You sound disappointed."

"I think I was." He polished off the rest of his beer. "Until today."

Turning to the bartender, he gestured for another bottle.

Liv's pulse accelerated. Taking another gulp of her drink, she tried not to act so giddy. It was hard, though. She was tipsy for the first time in ages—not to mention she wasn't supposed to be drinking while on her meds. But there was a voice inside her saying otherwise. Trying to justify not only her secret meeting but her new addiction: feeling wanted.

You never have a moment for yourself, Liv thought. *For once, you deserve something . . . you deserve this.*

The bartender dropped a fresh one in front of Fred.

"What's so different about today?" Liv asked.

Fred grinned. "Well, to start with, we're both playing hooky . . ."

"Hooky," she laughed. "What year were you born?"

"What? That's what they call it."

Their chuckles eventually died down until they were replaced by a slightly uncomfortable silence. Liv's heart continued to race as she wondered what Fred seemed to be holding back.

"But if you want to know the *real* reason . . . it's the company."

He's so damn nice.

Liv looked down at her wedding ring.

But you're married . . .

"Are you hungry?" Fred asked.

She hated that question. She always felt like people who saw her eating habits and body type would just assume the truth: she could always eat. But when she glanced up from her ring and saw the care and excitement in Fred's eyes, she was strangely comfortable with the question.

"Just a little, I guess," she lied.

"What do you say we have a late lunch?"

Looking down at her watch, she grimaced. "Oh, I don't know . . . I'm gonna have to be getting home pretty soon."

"C'mon, work wouldn't get out for another couple of hours anyway. Live a little." He smiled. "That's your name, isn't it?"

While such a name seemed ill-suited for a woman who normally had zero social life, she couldn't deny that Fred was right. She could either go and hit the McDonald's drive-thru and wallow in her misery before returning home to deal with whatever the issue of the day was, or she could get something to eat with Fred. A man who clearly cared about her and her well-being.

Fred watched her closely as he removed his wallet and called for the tab. There was a quiet confidence about him—like he already knew the answer she was about to give.

"It's just food, nothing to be stressed about," he explained, plucking some cash from his wallet.

Liv didn't want the fun to stop, but there were so many responsibilities weighing on her. And for once, she decided it didn't matter. She threw back the rest of her vodka spritz, set the glass on the bar, and smiled wide.

"Why not."

STIFF

When Bruce took his headphones off and wiped the cum from his belly, his cock was still stiff. He set the tissue under some paperwork in the trashcan beside another soiled Kleenex.

The first time Bruce had jerked off, he was beating his dick like a speed-metal drummer. He had to go at it so hard and long to cum that he wouldn't have been surprised if he bruised himself. Watching so much porn and becoming suffocated by constant fantasy left him in a strange place sexually. The desensitization was definitely a real thing. Despite stroking his cock until it was nearly bleeding, he was always ready for round two.

But now that he'd completely drained all the nut from his body, he needed a break. His little workout sessions had also made him work up an appetite. Adjusting his still-hard cock back into his pants, he zipped up.

Maybe I'll see if there's any more frozen burritos, he thought.

Bruce quickly snuck a peek at his work email, but with nothing new in the queue, he stood. As he unlocked the office door, he listened carefully. He hoped that Dustin was still in his room—if he wasn't, Bruce would just return to his office until the downstairs area was empty.

He didn't hear any evidence that Dustin was nearby. Happy with that revelation, Bruce stepped out of his office with a smile on his face.

Until he saw what lay at the foot of the stairs.

Spud's motionless body looked like it was frozen stiff. His arms were outstretched, and the grim look on his face ripped Bruce's heart and guts out all at once.

Bruce rushed up to Spud, crumbling to the ground.

"Oh, God! Spud! What . . . what the fuck?!"

He felt helpless and confused. The devastation sank in like the tip of a meat hook being set deep in his ribcage, and there was no getting it out. There was nothing he could do to change the sick reality before him.

His best friend was dead.

LATE LUNCH

Fred spread Liv's lips wide, using his tongue to toy around with her clit. Some of the motions teased, while others landed, making her squirm and moan. The intensity and passion he devoured her with was something she could've only dreamt about.

As he inserted his finger into her pussy, he let his lips fall to her asshole. Breathing heavily, Fred used his wet tongue to lap her crack and dance around the hole as his fingers continued to slide in and out of her.

Liv slapped her hand over her mouth, unsure if Fred's neighbors might hear. As her pelvis bucked, the feelings of ecstasy and anxiety battled inside her.

When Fred had asked if she wanted to have a late lunch, she figured they'd be going to a restaurant. When he explained he'd like to cook for her, she should've known that the only lunch he was planning on was the one he was having between her legs right then.

Jesus, what am I doing? Liv thought.

As she held her leg back to spread herself wider, Liv caught the glimmer from her wedding band in the corner of her eye. Part of her wanted to push Fred off her and explain that it was all a big mistake.

But there was another part that wanted him to start fucking her already.

The mental tug-of-war was ruining her experience. She forced the thoughts of Bruce and her life with him out of her mind and allowed herself to be free.

It's too late. It's already happening, she reasoned.

As the licking and fingering grew more intense, she couldn't take it anymore. Liv moaned with excitement before finally finding the courage to command him.

"Put it inside me . . . please," she begged.

Fred plunged his fingers deeper, pulling his boxers down with the other hand. "Is that what you want, baby?"

"I don't want it . . . I fucking *need* it," Liv wailed.

As she felt the hard cock enter her wet pussy, her legs started to tremble. He worked it into her slowly at first, but as she started to soak his rod, it was clear he couldn't resist the urge anymore. She could tell that he needed to have it. And she loved knowing it.

Liv let herself go, grabbing onto the headboard to stay in position as Fred let a few moans of pleasure escape. It didn't sound like he was even trying to be loud, which turned her on even more. She liked knowing that he couldn't control himself—that she felt *that* good to him.

The thrusts grew more primal, his hips clapping against Liv's thighs and the bottom of her ass. She kept one hand on the headboard while slipping the other down to her clit. As she toyed with herself, the pounding intensified.

"Fuck me," Liv whispered. "Fuck me harder."

Fred seemed to take the challenge seriously. Grunting, he grabbed hold of her hips and slung Liv onto her belly. He elevated her ass in the air and slipped his cock back inside her. Reaching forward, he took hold of Liv's hair and pulled back, working his dick deeper.

Normally, the first thing Liv would've thought about was her hair loss. She would've jumped to all the worst emotions. But with Fred, she didn't feel uncomfortable or embarrassed.

She didn't care if he pulled a big clump of hair right out of her head. The only thing she was thinking about anymore was cumming.

As his hips bucked, just knowing that he was about to blow his load brought her there. Building to climax, Liv's pleasure finally peaked, and a feeling of euphoria exploded between her legs.

They both moaned as Fred pulled out. When Liv felt the hot ropes of cum start to cover her back, the intensity of her orgasm was already beginning to even out. As she came down, the ecstasy was soon replaced by a more familiar emotion. The unease that she felt for the better part of every day unpacked itself inside her belly. Except now, the emotion was amplified tenfold.

What the fuck have I done?

"Goddamn," Fred said, falling to the free side of the bed.

"Can you grab me a towel?" Liv asked.

Fred turned on the TV. "The bathroom's right there. Get it yourself."

Liv was taken aback by his curtness. Suddenly, once the sex was over, his tone and attitude did a total one-eighty.

As he picked up his phone and started to scroll, the television rambled on in the background.

". . . and be sure to stick around later tonight, after local news and sports, as Fox premieres the all-new documentary, *Savage*. This original film will shed light on the Cumberland Caveman Killer and expose never-before-seen details on the grisly case that not only rocked a small New England town but—"

Liv's ears were distracted from the disturbing promo, perking up at the sound of a phone vibrating. She glanced over at her purse on the nightstand, and her gut sank. A terrible feeling came over her, and she had no idea why. The light from the front of the screen bled through the cloth of the bag. Cum still covering most of her back, Liv moved over and lifted the phone out of her purse. When she saw Bruce's name, fear and guilt instantly rattled her. She didn't dare answer it.

After allowing it to go to voicemail, her heart smashed furiously inside her chest—even more furious than when Fred was fucking her. Liv brought the phone into the bathroom and closed the door. As she grabbed one of the towels and started to wipe the semen off her back, she looked down at the screen. The voicemail indicator showed one message from Bruce.

Jesus . . . he never calls me when I'm "at work" unless it's bad.

Liv thought back to recent events. Dustin had just tried to burn the school down. She knew that she needed to listen to it right away.

She pressed the play button.

When Liv put the phone against her ear, it felt like a dagger going through her heart. The inhuman howl that Bruce let out wasn't even recognizable. He was so upset that the words were completely lost in the hurt. The heartbreaking message made her feel like she might vomit. She'd never heard Bruce so upset. The closest thing Liv could equate it to was the horrible reaction she'd had when they'd found her mother's corpse.

DOUBTS

Pressing his cell to his ear with one hand, Bruce listened. His gaze shifted from the computer monitor on his desk that read *Scituate Animal Shelter* to the pair of noise-canceling headphones before falling on the dog crate with the shroud over it.

Bruce's eyes glimmered.

"Again, I'm terribly sorry for your loss, Mr. Huxley," a woman's voice replied. "If you do decide that cremation is the proper route for Spud, we would be happy to assist you promptly."

Bruce wiped a teardrop from the corner of his eye. "Thank you."

"Best wishes," she said.

When the line disconnected, a feeling of fragility and sickness took hold of him. As the grief churned in Bruce's gut, the tears escaped him in bunches. He reached into the bottom drawer of his desk and retrieved a pill bottle.

He promptly extracted a single tablet, broke it in half, and swallowed it. These particular antidepressants always made him feel dead inside, but that was still better than dealing with life. Bruce shook his head and groaned.

Sometimes, when things got *really* messy, he took a double dose. It gave him the extra deadness required to remain calm and collected. It helped dull the effects of the carousel of disturbing events that constantly rotated around him at all times.

As of late, Bruce found himself dipping into his reserve stash often. The urge was constantly striking him, and now, just like all the other times, in that instant, he listened to the voice of reason.

Just another half to take the edge off, he thought. Bruce looked at the silent cage that contained his best friend's carcass. *I can't fucking deal with this right now.*

Just after Bruce was told that his son had been expelled from the Carter School, he'd collected the spit in his mouth and swallowed a half in the hallway waiting for Liv to leave the principal's office.

You're keeping me from exploding.

He thought about how the extra pill had served its purpose on the car ride, but when they'd arrived home, it did nothing to pacify the situation or stop the whipping he'd put on Dustin.

Maybe I should double up.

He didn't fight the idea, promptly swallowing the other half, praying that it would give him enough deadness to get him through what came next.

After he'd seen Spud lying lifeless in front of the stairs, he couldn't help but wonder.

Did Dustin have anything to do with it?

The urge to beat the boy senseless—ten times worse than the whipping he'd given him after being expelled— surfaced. The pity he'd felt for him just days ago no longer existed. Deep down, his instincts screamed.

He *knew* Dustin had something to do with it.

Is this medication even working?

The image of his shaking hand clenching his belt and whipping Dustin's ass flashed in his mind.

Is it what pushed me over the edge? Is that why— No, I need it. The pills are all that's keeping me in line. It probably would've been even worse without them.

He forced the questions about his chemical crutch out of his mind and allowed it to drift elsewhere.

What the fuck took Liv so long, and why didn't she answer her work phone?

Even when she'd called him back, it was from her cell. She was always on edge, but today she sounded different. Almost talking too much, like she was extra nervous about something.

Maybe it was just my message about the dog that rattled her. Can't be the easiest thing to hear through voicemail . . .

When she returned home and consoled him with a hug, the tips of her hair were damp. Bruce was too distraught to ask her, but now that he'd had a moment to settle down, the detail really bothered him.

Did she really leave me at home with Dustin and go out and fuck someone else while our dog died?

As suspicion surged in his mind, he frowned. So many things at the house felt off—more off than normal—and Bruce wanted someone to blame.

Well, if she did . . . one way or another, I'll find out.

GUILT OVER GRIEF

Liv wanted nothing more than to fall asleep. To be whisked away by the sandman to a fictitious place. A place where anything was possible. A place where things such as simple happiness, or even just emotional neutrality, didn't require backbreaking labor to achieve.

But simple comforts like peaceful slumber had become a rare commodity in recent years. She had once been a fiery spirit with a battery that was always full. But since motherhood, she'd begun to decay. The energy that was once limitless she now struggled to conserve. Even though her sleep was fractured and the nightmares wormed their way in, she took comfort in knowing that none of it was real. She could deal with that easier than the real-world fears. Getting in bed was easy, but getting out?

That was another story.

While she lay on her side in the darkness, back to the door, she wondered when Bruce might join her. The guilt was already feasting on her since he'd locked himself in his office a short time after she'd gotten home. Several hours had passed, and she still hadn't heard a peep.

Part of her worried that she was acting strange. When she'd returned and comforted Bruce over Spud, she'd felt horrible. And when she wasn't feeling good, it was obvious.

Hope I wasn't acting weird, she thought. *I can't believe Spud's gone . . . he's really gone.*

Sobbing, Liv realized that she'd been acting selfishly. More concerned about blinding her husband with lies than the death of their sweet dog. Still, her thoughts raced away from Spud seconds later.

It's not my fault. Bruce drove me away.

Demonizing her husband was easy enough—he gave her many legitimate reasons. Liv had already justified the affair in her head several different times since it happened. But as she continued to consider all the factors, she landed on her typical self-loathing judgments.

If I wasn't so fucking fat, he'd want to fuck me. If I could just stop the binging and do some goddamn exercise, none of this would've had to happen!

She'd never been able to get past how she looked since giving birth. Once Dustin slid out of Liv, her body never revisited its original shape again. She hadn't found a way around the never-ending exhaustion of being a mother. And due to the extra attention her son required, she knew recapturing her original form might never happen.

Those old pictures hurt to look at. It was like staring into a parallel dimension.

He's always on his phone and isolating himself. Wouldn't be surprised if he beat me to the punch and cheated first.

One of the things that bothered her most was Bruce's obsession with his phone. He was always checking it, morning, noon, and night. How many times had she woken up to see the screen's reflection bouncing off his pupils? While his job required him to be on-call and constantly monitor emails, she couldn't help but consider what else he might be monitoring.

Is he monitoring tits and ass?

She'd caught him doing so a few times before. Liv had enough concerns and Bruce had enough of an addiction that she felt compelled to find out. His social media search history showed the accounts of sexy, athletic types—just like she used to be.

While it hurt to know he was eyeing other women, she couldn't say that she hadn't done the same with the opposite sex. It might not have even mattered if they still fucked. If they fucked, her confidence wouldn't be in the pits. If they fucked, she'd know that he still wanted her, and the compliments of Fredson Dennard wouldn't have resonated with her so much.

Fred . . .

He'd kind of acted like a dick after they'd finished fucking. After the interaction and slight awkwardness post sex, a new question arose.

Was everything he said at the office and at the bar just a bunch of fancy lip service?

She didn't want to believe that. He'd spoken with such kindness and sincerity. Maybe she was just being too sensitive. It wasn't fair to cast judgment after one callous comment and some awkward silence.

Almost on cue, the phone on her nightstand buzzed. Liv snagged it and looked at the new text message.

Today was fucking incredible, Fred wrote. *I already can't wait for next time.*

Liv was both excited and terrified by the message. It clearly wasn't just fancy lip service if he was texting her the same day. But on the other hand, she hadn't even considered hooking up with him again. She'd already decided on the drive home that fucking Fred was just an awful, selfish, one-time mistake.

It was really *fucking good, though . . .*

She was quick to flipflop but didn't make any kind of decision. It seemed the cloud of confusion looming over her wasn't forecasted to clear up any time soon. Hesitating, she finally replied.

I have to agree, she wrote. *See you tomorrow.*

After she sent him a winking smiley face, Liv thought back to when she'd snooped through Bruce's phone. The inspection as a whole yielded little for Liv aside from the additional flurry of bruises to her ego.

It didn't appear that Bruce was into anything too serious. Just ogling internet randoms. His chats and texts were clean. But that still hadn't solved the problem, and deep down, she continued to wonder if he was hunting for her replacement.

Part of it's the stress Dustin creates . . . but how much?

Despite the uncomfortable nature of her son's dark side, Liv continued to try and convince herself that the incidents they'd witnessed were just part of a phase. No matter how tumultuous things got, she reminded herself that he was still in the early stages of development.

Of course, she still had her worries. Would her son do something so terrible that there would be no salvaging things—no fixing him? The recent incident in the basement also made her wonder if he was capable of hurting himself.

Still, Liv felt there was plenty of time to mend Dustin's behavioral issues. She'd tried to remind Bruce that there was still a chance, that their optimism shouldn't be dead. But he seemed to have a different perspective.

She'd watched the way Bruce looked at Dustin. Slowly deteriorating from a hopeful gaze to a gawk of disgust. It was as if his verdict was already set. That was just like Bruce. He was a know-it-all. Stubborn. And clearly, he already knew how their story was set to end.

Has he stopped loving me—?

Before she got a chance to decide, Liv's thought was interrupted by the sound of the door creaking open.

Liv promptly deleted the text and switched her phone to silent. Listening to Bruce disrobe and set his clothing on the dresser, she slid the phone under her pillow. Moments later, she felt the covers on her side move ever so slightly as he slipped into bed. He kept his distance, and she felt him turn onto his side so that their backs were facing each other.

Liv had been biting her lip since he entered the room, but it didn't take long for her to loosen the pinch.

"So, what happened?"

There was a long pause.

"Spud's in the crate . . . for now," Bruce replied.

"And?"

"And I guess that's where he's gonna stay until I take him to the oven."

Liv's lip trembled. "Oh . . . I'm sorry that you had to find him that way. I know how much you loved him. It's . . . just not going to be the same without him."

"Interesting."

"What is?"

"You just—you don't seem very upset." Bruce had a hint of disgust in his tone.

"Of course I'm upset—we've had Spud since before we were married. I'm devastated."

"Sure you are."

Liv turned to look at Bruce, but he didn't move. "What are you even saying?"

"I'm saying you didn't shed one tear for that dog you say you loved so much. You say you're devastated . . . but I just don't see it."

"Well, excuse me. I've got a husband who locks himself in his office every night, and the few minutes of the day he is actually present, he can barely speak to me without getting annoyed. I've got a son who assaults another kid in our house, then tries to kill himself"—she pointed to her chest—"and *I'm* the fucking one who goes and stays with him in the hospital. Then—"

"Sure, you do it all."

"I'm not done—*then*, when he gets released, he tries to burn his goddamn school down. So now, I'm stressed to the limit, spending all day trying to figure out how to get him placed or find help, swallowing pills like a test subject just to be able to get out of fucking bed every morning, and you're wondering *why* I'm emotionally broken?"

His only response was a heavy sigh.

Liv could hear the hatred and aggravation in Bruce's sigh. It was so abundant.

There was nothing she desired more than to see her husband smooth back out into the man she remembered from decades past. But now it wasn't just about Bruce any longer. Liv could feel her own rage and resentment starting to crackle louder, and there was no sign of the fire going out.

"Fuck you, Bruce," she whispered before turning back in the other direction. "Fuck you."

DOWN AND OUT

Bruce sat in his car outside the animal clinic, heartbroken. Staring at the cage with the cloth over it in the passenger seat, he shook his head. He thought about how much he would miss the feeling of Spud's soft coat rubbing against him, his chocolate eyes begging for another treat, and taking him for walks in the morning. But more than the cute stuff, he'd miss the companionship that Spud offered him. There was never any judgment—just love. Which was more than he could say about the other members of his family.

He made her aware of his decision but didn't give Liv an opportunity to be there. Since she hadn't reacted in the same manner as him, he assumed that attending Spud's cremation wasn't something on her mind anyway. Bruce's bond with the dog was stronger than Liv's, and so sending Spud off properly was of the utmost importance to him.

Dustin was an emotional chameleon. The reactionless boy made Bruce highly suspicious as to the extent of his involvement—if he had any—with Spud's death. Strangely enough, he hadn't even asked how the dog had died—a question Bruce believed would probably be the first thing out of the boy's mouth if he had nothing to do with it. But instead, there was only silence.

Hmm . . . he was like that after Alice too . . .

He vividly recalled how Dustin had sat on the couch while his mother broke down into hysterics. There was no consoling, no questions. Bruce viewed it as an unnatural reaction. Strange for a child to simply accept death without fear or curiosity.

Eyes widening, Bruce believed he may have finally connected the dots—or at least two of them.

That house . . . things were never the same after we stayed there. Might be something to that.

Shifting his attention back to the dog, Bruce looked from the entrance back to Spud's cage, debating.

Why does life have to keep bleeding me dry?

He never imagined this was what family life would be like. They had the white picket fence, financial stability, and any personal possessions one could dream of. But the mental and emotional elements were such a disjointed mess.

Bruce pictured his lovely wife with the same toned frame that had slapped against his thighs in their old apartment. With the same sexy confidence as when she'd wrapped her fingers around his cock. But now, Liv was a shell of her former self.

Not only was he uninterested in her body, but she depressed him. The constant worry, self-doubt, and shyness that he hadn't seen since their first date was too much. And even during the rare moments when her personality warts seemed to subside, she did something that, upon asking for her hand in marriage, he never thought possible.

She bored him.

She relegated him to a combination of internet fantasies and pathetic computer porn.

But is that her fault or my own?

He remained torn by the question.

On the other side of the coin, Bruce had always pictured having a son with morals and intelligence. A son who would only help their family name further blossom with respect, honor, and dignity.

While most of Dustin's more disturbing acts had been kept close to the vest, if the boy kept on his current path, there would be nothing powerful enough to cover the stench of shame and disappointment he'd tarnish them with.

Bruce continued to caress the shroud over Spud's crate. When Liv was first pregnant, he'd imagined his son would be as obedient as his dog. Instead, he might've killed him.

Tears started to form in the corners of Bruce's eyes.

You were the only one I could relate to. You deserved better, buddy. Much, much *better.*

The decision had been made. Bruce put the car in reverse and pulled out of the parking lot.

A SIGHT FOR SAD EYES

The sun seemed like it was setting faster each evening. Aside from the green desk lamp and glow of the computer screen, the house was filled with darkness. Liv hated the absolute calm around her. With Spud gone and Bruce away, it was *too* quiet. Yelling at him before bed the prior night hadn't really changed what she felt inside.

The stark silence was unnerving and distracting. She opened another tab in the browser, ready to search for some background music, when she heard it.

Thump!

The noise came from upstairs. It sounded like something or someone had fallen.

Liv jumped up from her chair.

"Dustin?"

She crept out of the living room to the front of the staircase.

"Are you okay?"

No response.

She flipped the light switch on the wall, but there was no reaction. The darkness remained.

"What the hell?"

She listened closely as she continued up the stairs.

Moving down the dark hall, drawing closer to Dustin's door, she heard a horrible choking noise. As the noise wormed about inside her head, Liv's stomach felt like it was about to fall out of her body.

"Dustin, what's going on?!"

There was still no response as Liv flung the door open.

In the darkness, backlit only by a sliver of moonlight slicing in from the window, Dustin's pale, naked body dangled. The backside of his frame faced her, hanging from a length of rope as he slowly turned like a rotisserie chicken being cooked alive.

Stunned, Liv watched the massive shadow outlined on the wall beside her moving chaotically as an arm flapped about at the waist. When her eyes darted back from the unsettling shadow to her son, she screamed. Dustin's face had turned purple, his eyes bugging out of his skull and drool pouring from his mouth. It was then that Liv realized what the purpose of his hand motion was.

Between his hips, in place of the standard male anatomy, was a bare corncob. The pith Dustin stroked so excitedly, stripped down and covered in chunks of vomit. She looked up into his glossy eyes while the teardrops rained. As his violet lips bubbled over with saliva, the sound of his choking grew louder than Liv's screams.

THE ROLODEX

"Shit!" Liv squealed, lifting her head off the desk.

The dream was vivid enough that her heart pumped furiously, and she felt a stabbing pain in her chest. The constant poor sleep—or lack thereof—was catching up with her. She was breathing like she'd just run a marathon.

The nightmares weren't new, but they'd never been as vile as what she'd just experienced. The more common ones involved the eerie, oversized shadows—similar to the ones her medication had her seeing around the house. The panic in her body still had her on pins and needles as the idea of losing her son throbbed in her mind.

I just want him to be okay, she thought.

She remembered ushering him to bed several nights prior. The look on his face when he'd lain down made it seem like he wasn't even there—a vacant stare, as though his mind was running but no one was behind the wheel.

Shuddering, Liv recalled what she'd seen in the hallway upon leaving his room. The fright generated by the thing in the darkness had immobilized her, its unsettling ebony outline sparking terror inside her before vanishing. But she was even more frightened after Bruce had explained that it wasn't him.

It was there one second and then gone the next . . . What the hell was that?

Whatever it was had started to get inside her head. Not only was she revisiting the memory in her nightmares but also daydreaming about it. The bizarre, detail-less shape was a vision she couldn't let go of.

The bottle sitting on the desk beside her was almost empty. She squinted at it while mashing the keyboard. "Can Xanax make you hallucinate?" suddenly occupied the search bar. She hit the enter key and skimmed the info.

Other changes may be more unusual and extreme. Side effects may include brain fog, hallucinations—seeing, hearing, or feeling things that are not there—suicidal thoughts, confusion, worsening of depression, and unusual excitement, nervousness, or irritability. Consult your clinician immediately if experienced.

She considered calling her doctor but dismissed the idea. *Got enough to deal with already. Don't need to be switching medications on top of it. Just deal with it. Whatever it is, it's not real.*

Liv shook her head from side to side, still trying to calm herself. She was supposed to be searching to find help for Dustin but was thinking about herself instead. Opening the bottle, she extracted a pill.

Of course it's not real.

She opened a new browser page and searched for "The Rolodex." As she examined the results, she found herself scrolling quite a bit before finally clicking on the one that seemed like the obvious choice: "The Rolodex: Medical Assistance Made Easy."

That sounds exactly like what Justine was talking about.

When the page loaded, there wasn't much other than a simple image of an outdated rolodex. The card displayed was blank, with a search bar overlayed in the center. Inside the search box were the faded instructions: *Enter Keywords & Symptoms.*

Liv keyed in the words "mentally unstable, aggressive tendencies, behavioral help." When she clicked the search button, the rolodex spun with a noise that sounded like paper flipping.

The card reappeared, blank again, this time the faded letters reading: *Zip Code.* After quickly firing off the digits, Liv pressed enter.

The rolodex cycled for several more seconds before producing an unexpected result. It wasn't so much the result itself that was unexpected, just that there was only one. She quickly expanded the profile and reviewed the details.

Marta Romero—I'm a Cognitive Behavioral Therapist (CBT) who specializes in child therapy. It is my belief that the most vital part of the three-pronged approach, CBT, is the patient and therapist connection. My goal is to create a calm, safe space, free of judgment for your child, to examine aspects of their life and determine the root of their distress.

I work together with the child and the parents to identify the appropriate methods to help your loved one find inner peace and balance. I have over fifteen years of experience working with adolescents and families who have battled anxiety, detachment from reality, low self-esteem, ADHD, severe trauma, emotional regulation issues, violent tendencies, rage bouts, and more. I previously worked at a mental institution for twelve years and have been providing in-house client care for the last several after opening my own private practice.

The expertise she noted sounded like *exactly* what Dustin needed. Marta didn't seem like the type to rattle. Judging from the laundry list of explosive symptoms she had direct experience with, this was precisely the type of person who could potentially remedy their conundrum, and maybe even Dustin's issues as a whole.

But as Liv scanned and scrolled, desperately looking for the contact information, her heart sank.

Accepting waitlist patients only at this time.

"Damn!" Liv slapped the laptop base. "Why can't anything just be easy?"

"The fuck is it now?" Bruce asked.

The unexpected interruption caused Liv to whip around. Standing in the entrance of the living room, shrouded in darkness, was her husband's unmistakable slumped posture with the outline of a rectangular whiskey bottle filling one hand.

Bruce dropped onto the couch, put the bottle to his lips, and chugged. The bitter taste of the bourbon made him wince while he awaited his wife's response.

Liv watched Bruce's broken body language and instantly felt like a horrible person. Having had a little time to think about everything—including cheating on him—she felt sorry. Knowing how close he had been with Spud, she could understand him being angry.

She rubbed her hands against her legs anxiously. "How did everything go with—?"

"I don't wanna get into it," Bruce interrupted.

Liv nodded. "I understand."

"I don't think you do." Bruce shook his head and then took another gulp. "I . . . I couldn't burn him. I decided I'll give him a formal burial . . . here."

"Okay," Liv whispered.

Bruce struggled but was able to corral his tears.

She bit her lip, imagining her face looking almost as zombie-ish as her husband's as they exchanged overly medicated stares.

"Whatever you think is best, I support it," she said.

Bruce slurred his words as he finished another swig. "You know . . . in a way, it's good. He's definitely in a better place now." He gestured to the ceiling with his eyes. "But enough about me. What're you all worked up about?"

Liv rubbed her forehead with her fingers. "I found this great home therapist. She's the only one that came up in the stupid search who was in our range and really matches what we need."

"But?" Bruce asked.

"She's not accepting new patients right now."

Bruce sniffed and grinned. "Like hell she isn't."

Liv furrowed her brow.

"You know, there's one thing in this world that people always seem to find time for." Bruce held a single finger up in the air. "And it's the *one* thing we have a decent amount of . . ."

She took some relief in Bruce being eager to figure out a way to move past the roadblock.

". . . but even all the money in the world would be absolutely worthless to us until we find a way to fucking fix him."

Liv understood the inference but wasn't as sure as Bruce was. "So, what do you want me to do?"

Bruce tapped his wedding band nervously against the bottle and took another mouthful. "Tell her that we'll give her a thousand dollars for an in-person meeting."

THE ARRIVAL

Marta Romero drove down the dark road, only having a partial idea as to what she was getting ready to walk into. Her services were posted on many internet sites, and so a certain amount of embellishment by potential clients was always expected. But there were certain things in the email from the Huxleys that made it stand out—qualities different than most requests.

For one, she'd never gotten a message offering to pay out a grand for a single meeting.

They must be loaded, Marta thought.

Secondly, the sheer honesty of the email was beyond what most people cared to divulge—especially from a family so seemingly desperate. Usually, the potential-client emails were heavily sugarcoated. It was only after she arrived and investigated that she peeled back the layers and uncovered the true delinquency she'd be up against.

While the child's foul language, perverse mind, interest in fire, and his potential for suicidal tendencies were all classic properties of psychotic behavior, it was nothing new. They were all traits that Marta had been required to face at various junctures of her career.

The obsession with choking is a bit different . . . Not sure I've encountered that before.

She wasn't frightened by the bizarre nature of the details in the email. Quite the contrary—she was excited.

This could be it. This could finally be the one that sends me into early retirement.

In an industry such as children's behavioral therapy, one had to have thick skin. Screams, tantrums, and acts of utter insanity were the standard. As her headlights lit up the long driveway, one thing was certain: she'd be leaving the meeting richer than when she'd arrived. But exactly how much richer was up for debate. The potential for a major salary increase gave her a natural high.

Let this finally be the one.

The family's obvious desperation could also be used as a tool during negotiations. People didn't typically ask to meet on a weeknight, especially after the sun had already gone down. The request was written in such a way that they sounded like they might've been willing to pay double just to get her there. Such a thought had crossed her mind even when she was reading the email initially.

Don't rush it. She felt a smile tightening her face. *The best things come to those who are patient.*

As the car came to a stop in front of the big house, the darkness wasn't enough to conceal the charm of the property. Marta's eyes popped—she was stupefied. It was the kind of house that someone like her could've only dreamt of living in.

This is a good sign . . .

She stepped out of the car and took in the regal architecture. From the beautiful Palladian window at the front of the house to the flowering lilac tree in the center of the circular driveway, it was all quite picturesque. A collection of gorgeous things she'd never been fortunate enough to experience. Luxury the likes of which she'd only been teased with upon visiting her patients.

The area was isolated, all but for the screech of crickets. A flash in the window upstairs caught Marta's eye. She looked up at the second floor.

Through the glass, beside a glowing lamp, stood a young boy with fiery hair. The child's glare was wicked, instantly causing a shiver to run down her spine. The illumination cast an abnormal shadow in the background—an eerie outline that spread every which way and occupied most of the child's room.

Marta could no longer contain her excitement.

It's true.

MONEY TALKS

When Bruce opened the door, he was a bit fidgety. But the sparkling eyes of the olive-skinned woman on his doorstep evened him right out. She was not what he'd expected. She looked much younger and more beautiful than he would've imagined for a woman of such experience.

Holy hot yoga, Bruce thought, looking her up and down. There was something about the woman that made him tingle inside. *She kind of reminds me of Natalia Nuñez.*

As Marta reached toward him, he noticed that her plum nail polish matched her lipstick—such a deep shade that it was almost as black as her eyeshadow.

"You must be Mr. Huxley," she said.

As Bruce looked her over, his jaw hung slightly. He knew what he wanted to say yet remained mum. Her presence felt different, almost powerful. He shook her hand, their skin touching for what he feared was longer than necessary.

"Call me Bruce," he finally managed.

"All right."

Bruce gestured ahead. "Please, right this way. My wife, Liv, is in the parlor. Thanks again for agreeing to meet us so late. We just figured it would be best to find a time when we could talk, just the three of us."

"Of course." She nodded. "I understand, and I also think it's best we talk before involving . . . Sorry, what was your boy's name again?"

"Dustin."

Bruce noticed that Marta was taking in the extravagant interior of the house. The regal furnishings, state-of-the-art electronics, and modern yet homey décor, he knew, were lovely.

"Dustin . . ." she said, trailing off while getting lost in the lavish surroundings. "And considering the generous sum you and your wife have been kind enough to offer me, it's no trouble at all."

Liv rose from the couch to greet Marta at the entrance. Despite being just as jittery as her husband, Liv's handshake didn't linger.

"Thank you so much for coming," she said, furrowing her brow. "You look . . . young."

Marta squinted. "I suppose I was just fortunate enough to age with grace—so far anyway." She chuckled.

The moment was awkward, but Liv pushed on from it. "Can—can I get you a drink or something?"

Marta shook her head. "No, thank you, but I will take a seat if that's all right."

"Of course," Bruce and Liv chorused before taking their own seats on the couch across from her.

Marta sat in the recliner just a few feet away, looking at the various notebooks and envelopes stacked atop the glass coffee table.

"Your house is quite lovely, but something tells me those aren't part of the typical décor."

Bruce bit his lip.

As Liv cleared her throat, she stared at the big stack of paper produced strictly by mental illness. She stared at her fears. "We figured that it would be best to have something to show you . . . what kind of level he's on."

Bruce sensed discomfort and tension arising as the subject was broached. "Maybe we should talk a bit first and sort of work our way into those."

Marta ignored his suggestion, picking up the notebook on top of the pile and opening it. Her eyes widened as she flipped through the pages, stopping suddenly.

"Wow," Marta whispered.

Bruce squirmed on the couch. Part of him wondered if their potential savior was about to head for the hills.

A birthday card was wedged inside picturing a woman with bright red hair—like Liv's—with a rope wound around her neck and drool and blood oozing out of her mouth.

Marta opened the card and examined it carefully, reading it to herself.

"He—uh—he has quite the imagination," Bruce said.

"It appears so," Marta agreed. "Has he been officially diagnosed with anything?"

"More like everything," Bruce said.

Liv rubbed her hands together anxiously. "We've gotten a lot of . . . conflicting information. If it's okay with you, we'd almost rather just start fresh."

"Start fresh?" Marta asked.

"I mean, just have you evaluate him independently, not taking those prior opinions into account."

Marta flipped through a few more pages of the book. It was more of the same. A vile mixture of violence—mostly strangulation—and odd, sexually suggestive material. "*If* I'm able to evaluate Dustin—and that's still a big 'if'—I can assure you all of my conclusions will be drawn based on my own interpretations and interactions with him. I never rely on opinions from the past."

"That's good," Bruce said.

Marta stared deeply into Liv's fragile eyes. "May I ask you a question, Mrs. Huxley? Fair warning—it may be slightly uncomfortable."

Liv nodded without hesitation. "Whatever you need."

"Outside of this . . ." Marta pointed to the birthday card. "Has Dustin ever talked about or maybe attempted to hurt you? Physically, I mean."

"No," Liv replied.

Marta glared at her like a heartless statue. "Have you ever hurt him?"

A look of disgust and shock crinkled Liv's lips. It seemed like she wasn't prepared for the question.

"What do you mean? Of course not."

Bruce was caught off guard by the inquiry. He instantly thought back to the whipping he'd given the boy a few nights prior.

"Please understand," Marta said, "it is not my intention to offend you."

Bruce tried to grab hold of Liv's arm and calm her, but she shook him off, a snarl still contorting her face. "Then why would you ask such a thing?"

"I assure you, every question I ask is out of necessity." Marta pointed at the notebooks and birthday card. "And after reading the things you wrote in your email, my experience would lead me to infer that the boy might've witnessed some kind of deeply traumatic experience. And at his age, those types of events would typically stem from inside the household."

"Then ask that," Liv said. "Don't accuse me of hurting my son when you don't have a clue what I've sacrificed to try and save him."

"Certainly." Marta didn't bother hiding her smirk. "Let me rephrase the question. In regard to the root cause, and getting back to any potential trauma, is there anything at all either of you can think of?"

Liv squinted as Bruce scratched the side of his leg.

"Even if it's outside of your immediate family," Marta continued. "Is there anything, anything at all, that comes to mind? Maybe a concussion when he was young, or some kind of accident? I implore you both to think carefully. Sometimes, the smallest details can assist in uncovering viable solutions."

Liv exhaled slowly, glancing up at the ceiling, deep in thought. "I . . . I don't think so—"

"Well, there was that one thing," Bruce interrupted.

Marta seemed to pick up on the sheepishness in his tone. It seemed like she'd noticed that Bruce felt uncomfortable bringing it up.

"What are you talking about?" Liv asked.

"You know," Bruce whispered. "He was there, at the house, with your mother . . . when she . . ."

Bruce studied Liv's reaction. He could see an immediate shift—the discomfort was swelling inside her.

"That's true," Liv conceded. "But . . . Dustin was, like, four years old when my mother died."

"With respect," Marta said, "did he *see* her die?"

Liv shook her head.

"Well, technically, we don't actually know that for sure," Bruce corrected. "It seems likely he didn't, though . . . I suppose."

"I'm not going to lie, this thought has actually crossed my mind recently," Liv said

Mine too, Bruce thought.

He found it interesting that they both had come back around to what had transpired at Alice's house all those years ago. Maybe there was something to it—maybe he needed to think on it even more.

"It's just, he's never even spoken about it," Liv said. "I mean, not even once. He wasn't upset when it happened. If it affected him . . . then wouldn't he have spoken about it at some point?"

"Not necessarily," Marta said. "There are many cases of people severely impacted by traumatic events who don't open up until well into adulthood. It all depends on the person—we are all individuals. If you're willing to share what happened at your mother's house, it might help."

Bruce grabbed Liv's hand and whispered, "You don't have to."

"It's okay, I don't mind," Liv replied. She looked at Marta as if forcing herself to trust her. "I'll try anything if you think it will help."

"You're very brave," Marta said.

Liv nodded, searching for the words. "My mother died of a massive stroke in the cellar of her new house. On that day, we'd stayed over and helped her move in."

Bruce caressed Liv's hand, knowing how much that day had devastated her.

"Bruce and I were asleep in bed while my mother was in the living room watching a movie with Dustin," Liv continued. "Then, for some reason . . . she went into the basement. And . . . that's where we found her."

Marta stroked her chin in thought. "Interesting."

Bruce couldn't wait any longer. He'd been holding his cards, but that moment seemed like the best time to move in for the kill.

"Well, if you find *that* interesting, then I can only imagine what you'll think after getting to know us a little more."

Marta turned her attention to him.

"Let us hire you to work with him on weekdays," Bruce suggested. "You read the email. You know what a fucking nightmare this has been for us. Help us figure this out, once and for all."

Marta didn't blink. "I'm afraid it's not that simple—"

"Then let's make it simple," Bruce said, opening up his checkbook. "You make us your priority, and we'll make you ours." He wrote a one followed by three zeroes in the amount box. "If we can come to an agreement tonight, I left enough space to add another zero."

Marta narrowed her eyes at Bruce. He assumed that she enjoyed looking at him—not just because he was attractive but also because when she looked at him, she didn't see bullshit. He could walk the walk.

On the other hand, he could see that his better half didn't seem to be Marta's favorite person. At first glimpse, the two of them got along about as good as oil and water. But he knew Liv would deal with her if she could help them. Bruce felt what he was offering to Marta would be enough to push past any petty annoyances. With the experience she had, he was sure Marta had been in worse situations and dealt with them for far less money.

"I can add it right now," Bruce persisted, pen poised. "It'll be enough for you to maybe refer a colleague to your current patients and make us your primary focus. Just say the word."

The desperation in his voice was palpable. Bruce wondered if she might try to exploit it and negotiate harder. If she did, he would just have to give her more.

He didn't want Marta to feel like she'd just walked into a casino where every slot was set to strike, but at the same time, he wanted her to feel like if she played her cards right, this was just the first of many jackpots.

Marta hesitated, creating a tension that undoubtedly rattled the souls of the lost parents.

"Well?" Bruce pressed.

Marta nodded as a tight smile curled the corner of her mouth. "It's a deal."

RELUCTANT SLUMBER

Liv stared at the wall, a flux of emotions inside her, same as she did every night. When she felt the weight of Bruce's body finally fill the other side of the bed, she couldn't help but ask the question that had been on her mind since their meeting with Marta had finished.

"Do you think something happened to Dustin at my mom's house?"

Bruce sighed. "I think it would be best if we focus on the positives from tonight. We've got help. We've found someone who's going to take a lot of pressure off us, and maybe things around here will change over time. For the better, I mean. Besides, we can't change the past."

If it were only that easy, Liv thought.

He was right, though—there was no way to know, so it made no sense dwelling on such dark irrelevancies. Her eyes darted to the prescription bottle on the nightstand that was supposed to be negating such notions.

"Okay," she whispered.

She felt Bruce's lips on the back of her neck.

"Goodnight," he whispered.

For the first time in a while, that might've actually been the case. If Marta could hold up her end of the bargain, maybe it could even be a good week.

While something about Marta rubbed Liv the wrong way, she couldn't deny her many credentials. The woman's robust history of success in the fields of mental health and behavioral therapy were exactly what they needed. Marta also harbored a certain confidence that made Liv believe she might be the one to finally change things. She asked tough questions, but they were the right questions.

And besides, even if her record and aura hadn't been impressive, they had nowhere else to turn—Marta was it.

HERE TO HELP

Marta sat in the chair in Dustin's room while he colored in the drawing on his bed. This piece pictured a dachshund strung over a door, choking. The blood vessels in the dog's eyes were blown out of proportion. He etched further detail into the hard, red dog dick sliding out from the skin between its legs. As she watched him continue to fill in the color, Marta smiled.

Dustin's eyes darted up from the page. He seemed intrigued by her reaction.

"You find this amusing?" he asked, going back to coloring the picture.

"No harm in a little creative imagination," she said.

"Who said this was imagination?"

Marta raised an eyebrow. "You actually did that to someone's dog?"

Dustin looked at her with an icy stare. "He's *my* dog. Well . . . not anymore. Spud's dead now."

"So . . . you killed your dog?"

Squinting, Dustin shook his head. "Don't be silly." He pointed to the dog's erect cock. "He's not dead . . . just elsewhere."

"What do you mean?"

"I helped him be free," Dustin continued. "I helped him achieve the kind of pleasure that people obsess about but cannot understand."

"But he *is* dead, right?"

"He's transcended."

"To where?"

"An unseen place. A place that can't be explained, only experienced."

Marta scratched at her chin. "I find it interesting that you speak so eloquently. More so than any fourteen-year-old I've ever spoken to. Do you do this around everyone, or is it just because—"

"I do it for those who show genuine interest."

"Interest in what?"

"Achieving transcendence."

"So, what, the people who don't listen to what you have to say, you just don't bother with them?"

"Oh, I bother with them. I make life as agonizing as possible for them, in hopes that one day they'll see the truth. They don't realize that I'm trying to help them."

"I understand."

"Do you?" Dustin scoffed, eyes momentarily shooting up from his drawing.

"If you think I don't, then help me understand."

"Do you know what it's like to not feel?" Dustin gazed out the window at Marta's vehicle. "To be trapped inside a body that, truthfully, you're no more connected to than a driver is to their car. To have to live every fucking day in a world of fantasy that you can touch but not sense. And all the while, you have this information, this experience . . . It's only natural to want to live vicariously through others, wouldn't you imagine?"

Marta nodded, wanting him to continue.

"Right . . ." Dustin squeezed the colored pencil in his hand tight. "Because you know how good it can feel when you go right up to the edge. When you're just a half-breath away from the end."

The pencil snapped, but Marta didn't flinch.

"I'm not saying everyone has to push it as far as I did . . . But they're fools if they don't step up to the edge."

Dustin selected a new pencil and then returned to the drawing.

"How far did you push it?" Marta asked.

As Dustin finished his final few scribbles on the macabre illustration, his eyes lit up and locked on to Marta. It was like he wasn't used to people actually listening to anything he had to say.

"I transcended," he whispered through his grin. "I went past the point of no return and felt the turbulence of ultimate pleasure. Something that no one in this house would ever understand."

"I promise you, I'm not like them," Marta said.

"Are you saying that you're open to transcending? Open to my guidance?"

"I am. What you say speaks to me. I yearn to find a pleasure that can take me to where I need."

"I will show you," Dustin whispered.

"*But* . . . I'll need to know more in advance. You must understand that this is the first I've heard of it. To involve myself in something so risky frightens me. I would first need to build trust with you. Only so that I could then harness my fears and be able to fully give myself when I'm enlightened enough to participate."

"That's understandable," Dustin said.

Leaning over, Marta placed her hand on the drawing. "May I have this?"

"I'd like very much for you to have it. I can already tell that you appreciate it for what it actually is."

"Thank you kindly," she said, folding the piece of paper over several times before slipping it into her purse. "I must ask, are your parents aware that you were responsible for what happened to Spud?"

Dustin grinned and shook his head as he put away his colored pencils. "No, but I'm considering telling them."

"I see," Marta said. "I think this could be a good test for us. One way we can build trust would be by keeping secrets. If you can trust me to be the only one who knows what happened to your dog, then maybe I can trust you to . . ."

As she considered her word choice, she thought back to the birthday card's imagery and the language used inside.

Dustin leaned in, eager for her to continue.

"Then maybe I can trust you to show me how to choke," Marta whispered.

QUESTIONS

Bruce was wondering two things on the drive home: Did Dustin behave on his first day, and was Marta's cunt still tight? She didn't look like she'd had any children. After constantly dealing with the most defective kids society had to offer, it wouldn't have been a surprise.

She had no business having the type of toned body she flaunted at her age. Thick and fit—just the way he liked it. Her skin was a sexy bronze, and she put on just enough makeup for his taste. He might've found a replacement for the yoga girl he habitually jerked off to.

Fucking whore, he thought. *I bet she's a freak. I bet she takes it up the ass and eats it like ice cream.*

He adjusted his erection against the side of his pants. It was throbbing and ready at the thought of finding out. He was enthralled by the very fact that she'd taken the job. The money was well worth it—not only for Dustin's sake but to have a sweet piece of trim like that walking around.

There was an instant sexual tension that he'd felt between them. Marta was subtle about it, but Bruce could see it. The little jabs at his wife, questioning if she'd abused Dustin. He hadn't played the field in a while, but this was as obvious as an octopus in a swimming pool.

There was something there, and it excited him.

Ring! Ring!

Bruce took his eyes off the road as Liv's name and picture overtook the GPS screen. He exhaled, wondering what it could be about, before mustering the courage to answer the call.

"Hey," he said.

"Hi," Liv replied.

Bruce shifted an eyebrow upward. "What's up? Did everything go okay?"

"Yeah, Marta said it was fine. I was just wondering if you could pick something up for dinner on your way home. We're running a little low on groceries."

"What do you want?"

"Whatever's easy."

"Okay, then."

"All right, thanks. I guess I'll see you in a little bit, then . . . Love you."

Bruce paused. "I love you too."

As the call disconnected, he wondered why telling his wife he loved her was such a chore. It was getting harder each day, and that concerned him.

I do still love her, right?

Of course he did. Their relationship had just hit an insufferable patch. They were both stressed beyond explanation. Liv—in some ways, at least—was still the girl he remembered when they'd first met. The sweet, gentle soul that was the first person to ever make him feel at home anywhere as long as they were together.

Things were far from ideal between them, but they weren't irreparable. Sometimes he just had to remind himself. The deterioration of their once promising family unit had left a stain on their romance and lust for each other. But that could change.

That's why Marta was *actually* there—to fix all the fuckery, not to create more. But if it was going to work, Bruce couldn't walk around thinking the way he just had. The horndog in him needed to stay leashed.

All these thoughts . . . they're just that: thoughts. I'd never actually do anything with her. I'll just think about it and jerk off instead.

The depression, pressure, and drugs had led to a daily discombobulation that left Bruce's soul twisted. But now that he and Liv had some real hands-on support, the wallowing man he was would be a thing of the past. Maybe not overnight, but hopefully a short way down the road.

He shook his head side to side and swallowed. The pills had been making his mouth extremely dry as of late—one of their many side effects.

Keep your head on straight.

After collecting himself, he felt a bit better.

Until he remembered where he was heading.

AFTERTHOUGHTS

Liv listened intently, her leg nervously rocking up and down as she awaited further details. She carefully studied Marta and her mannerisms to see if she was trying to sugarcoat things.

She actually seems pretty calm, Liv thought.

Marta had her back to Liv, looking out the kitchen window at the driveway. "I'd say it went better than expected. He didn't exactly open up or anything, but I can see great potential already."

"Where is he?" Liv asked.

"He's just upstairs drawing."

Liv felt the wrinkles form on her forehead. "You . . . you mean he didn't say anything irregular or strange at all?"

"Not really. It was a rather straightforward conversation. It's possible he's just not comfortable with me yet, so he is masking the more obvious issues. It's not entirely uncommon. As I continue to work with him, I'm sure I'll get more specific details out of him."

"I suppose that's not completely out of character. He's had really good streaks of behavior around administrative or professional types. But he's been so erratic lately . . . I guess I'm just a little surprised."

"Well, that's a good surprise, isn't it?" Marta grinned.

Returning the smile, Liv nodded. "Do you mind if I ask what you talked about then?"

"Um . . . today, Dustin was mostly expressing to me some feelings of sadness."

"Really . . . Sad about what?"

"The death of your dog, Spud."

Liv did her best to keep herself together. She could've cried—that's how much it meant to her. A reason to hope was something she hadn't had in some time. Part of her didn't want to believe it—she'd been disappointed many times before—but maybe because it was coming from a new person, it made her give the idea more credence than she normally would have.

He's grieving. Finally, something good—a normal emotion.

"That's . . . wonderful," Liv whispered.

"I agree," Marta said. "And what's even more wonderful is that I'm confident you and Bruce are going to feel like you're in a completely different situation very soon."

"You have no idea how much that means," Liv said.

Marta looked out the window again. "Speaking of Bruce, where is he? It'd be great to share the progress with him too. I thought you said he was supposed to be home by now."

Marta's keen attention to her husband's whereabouts made Liv make a mental note.

What the hell does she care?

She instantly tried to reel herself in. The absence of intimacy in her marriage always gave her a tendency to get jealous over nothing.

Don't screw up a good thing. She's just here to help. Relax.

Liv rubbed the side of her face, convincing herself it was nothing. "He's just picking up some food for us on the way home."

"Oh," Marta replied. "I see."

The phone in Liv's pocket vibrated.

"Well, I guess I'll get going then," Marta said.

"All right." Liv nodded. "I'll see you tomorrow."

As Liv let Marta out the door, they exchanged smiles and goodbyes.

Liv watched through the glass window as Marta's headlights disappeared down the driveway, then quickly retrieved the phone from her pocket and unlocked it.

The text was from Fred. Feelings of giddiness and fear jousted inside her heart.

Can't stop thinking about cumming all over your back, Fred wrote. *I loved pulling your hair and hearing you moan, it just made me wanna fuck you harder. I just keep thinking about pushing you into the supply closet at work and bending you over. Needless to say, I didn't get a lot of work done today.*

The text left her flustered. She could feel an excited tingle below as she considered the office fantasy. But before she could get too into the specifics, a pair of headlights appeared in the distance.

"Shit," Liv mumbled as she rushed to delete the text.

MEMORIAL

When Bruce got out of the car, there was almost no daylight left. But he didn't want to wait any longer. Doing so would only prolong his pain and border on being disrespectful to Spud. He opened the hatch and took out the shovel and the baby sugar maple.

There was a spot at the front left of the house where there was enough space to plant it, and Bruce didn't waste any time. After a trip to the outdoor shed, he put the spade in the ground and started to dig. By the time he'd hollowed out a small hole, he heard the front door open.

"Planting something?" Liv asked, approaching him from behind.

"Yeah," Bruce replied, pausing and looking into the hole. Returning to his car, he removed the small, shrouded cage with Spud's corpse and set it in the hole in the ground. "I . . . I figure, this way, he'll always be here with us."

Liv crept up beside him and wrapped her arm around his waist. This was the part where she was supposed to get emotional, but the look in her eyes mirrored Bruce's—her medication was doing its job well.

"That's really sweet," she said. "It'll be good having him here. In a way, he'll live on."

"I'm glad you think so," Bruce whispered.

He got down on one knee, still contemplating.

"Here, I'll help you," Liv said, picking up the potted tree. It was a sizable sapling, so she had to lift with her legs.

Trying not to choke up, Bruce helped her maneuver the tree into the ditch, and they both pushed the pile of dirt around the edges.

"I miss him so damn much," Bruce said.

"I know, sweetie," Liv replied. "Me too."

She reached over, wrapping her arms around him.

Accepting her embrace, Bruce squeezed her tightly, sobbing as he turned away from the tree. It hurt too much to keep looking at it.

Instead, his watery eyes drifted to the house and, more specifically, the second-floor window. Dustin stared down at them with a blank expression.

THE VESSEL

Marta sat cross-legged on the cold, wooden floor with a weathered book cracked open in front of her. She held a beige dish in one hand and an icepick in the other. The shack wasn't much to look at, but she was grateful to have a place to stay and call her own. Money didn't just fall into her lap—it had always been hard-earned.

She looked at the picture of the middle-aged Hispanic man smoking a cigarette on the wall and shook her head. There had never been anyone in her life who had looked out for her; she'd always had to look out for herself. Growing up in the spare room not much larger than a closet, she'd had plenty of time to dream. But oftentimes she had to do it over the shouts of her drug-addicted uncle.

Uncle Andrés hadn't always been an addict. She remembered some less turbulent times when she was young. Her uncle's girlfriend, Carla, had kept him stable and happy, until she left one day—she just disappeared.

Blindsided, Marta had watched Uncle Andrés slowly unravel. The once clean house turned into a dump, and Uncle Andrés' straightedge ways grew warped. He experimented with many drugs, and before long, peaceful times in their home were over and the house had turned into a haven for homeless degenerates, prostitutes, and scummy streetfolk.

You've come a long way, Marta thought. *But not long enough.*

In the picture of Uncle Andrés, she could see her house in the background. At the time, the door of that awful place was open for anyone who had drugs, alcohol, or a pussy. Disturbed men stumbling into her room high out of their minds, horny, or a combination of the two was a normal occurrence.

It was inside the house where she'd seen violence for the first time—and just how effective it could be. A prostitute had rummaged through her uncle's room after he'd finished shooting up and passed out. When Marta heard the screaming in the kitchen, she peeked through the keyhole of her bedroom door.

The burner on the stove was red hot as Uncle Andrés grabbed the woman by the hair with one hand and held a battered hardcover book in the other.

"You filthy fuckin' whore," Uncle Andrés said. "You try to steal my mother's books? My mother would've died for those!"

Marta had watched, sobbing quietly, as Uncle Andrés pressed the hooker's face against the spiral stove burner. As she screamed and wiggled, the smoke rose off her face. But Uncle Andrés kept her pressed firm.

"Just because I don't know how to use it doesn't mean you can use them against me!" Uncle Andrés bellowed.

Eventually, some of the flesh on the screaming whore's face started to melt and her hair caught fire. When Uncle Andrés noticed her body go limp, he let her fiery head fall to the floor. Marta continued watching him as he stomped out smoky follicles until it was a bloody and broken mess.

Despite Marta's fear of her uncle, she figured those books must've meant something if he was willing to murder a girl in cold blood over them. While she knew there was a risk of ending up like the prostitute, Marta didn't care. She needed to know what was inside those books.

Thank you, Uncle Andrés. Without you, none of this is possible.

It took her several years to read the books and even longer to understand them. But sneaking in and out of Uncle Andrés' room while he was away eventually paid off. The knowledge she gained opened up another world for her. One where she didn't have to depend on a drug addict. And eventually, she grew old enough to put her plan into action.

The ritual she'd learned was easy enough.

Mindless self-indulgence, she recalled as she used the icepick to carve a spiral symbol into the bowl beside the book.

Back then, her uncle was already regularly shooting up. All the ritual had done was persuaded him to keep doing it. Loaded needle after loaded needle, Uncle Andrés didn't stop until he'd gotten three and a half tubes of juice in his veins.

Just a short time later, Uncle Andrés' house was now hers. It was no longer a filthy drug den but her sanctuary. And the local creeps who'd partied there for so long quickly learned to not bother her, for those who did always ended up on a path toward grave misfortune.

After clawing her way to inner-city stability, her teachings pointed her in the direction of the mental health industry. To get the attention of potential clients, she embellished—two years of experience turned into twelve.

There were things in the books that explained how many cerebral issues were deeply spiritual. But it was Marta who realized this wisdom and information could be used to create potentially lucrative opportunities.

Marta aspired to own more than Uncle Andrés' shack. She desired to acquire what Bruce and Liv had—or maybe more. Tired of picking up the scraps of others, she'd been preparing herself for a different life. The problem was such a unique opportunity couldn't just manifest overnight. But nonetheless, that opportunity had finally arrived.

They have no fucking clue what it's like, she thought. *But they'll learn. Once I have what I've worked all this time for.*

Marta couldn't stop herself from grinning.

Can't believe another one fell into my lap so quickly. Maybe there are just more than I assumed. Hopefully, there's enough that I'll soon be gone from this horrid place for good.

The Huxleys were stupid enough to lay all their cards on the table during their initial meeting—a decision Marta would most definitely make them pay for. The knowledge that she was their last resort was the mechanism that would help her bleed them dry.

As Marta used the icepick to finish scraping the final occultic symbol into the bowl, she looked up. From inside the massive, rusty birdcage, the white dove stared blankly at her. She traced her fingers over the dozens of orphic outlines scratched into the ceramic before standing. Marta approached the table beside the cage and set the dish and icepick down.

"Here, birdie birdie," she whispered, quickly opening the door to the huge cage and venturing inside to snatch the creature.

When she stared into the dove's darting eyes, Bruce came to mind. Marta saw similarities between the bird's eyes and his. There was a certain amount of fear in each of them. The kind of fear one attains when they're forced to put their trust in someone else. But that wasn't all she saw in Bruce's gaze. She saw excitement too.

Excitement that his stress might finally be relieved.

Excitement that she might mend his son's broken mind.

Excitement that something worth fucking was finally walking around his house again.

It made her feel good to know she was desired. In just the short time she'd been around him, Marta was already certain of it. There were tingles in her body when she thought about him. Such a handsome and naturally fit man. She could tell he was sex-starved and didn't want to see such deliciousness continue to be wasted.

Who knows . . .?

She twisted the dove's neck sideways until a sickening crack echoed throughout the room.

Maybe this'll work out well for both of us.

There was something about a man who was a bit older and had his affairs in order that stuck out to Marta. The chaos and general dysfunction she'd been raised around might've had something to do with it. There was something about stability that was sexy to her.

A loud pounding caught Marta off guard, making her jump. Eyebrow raised, she set the dead dove down, left the spare room, and made her way to the front door.

"Who is it?" Marta asked.

The stern voice on the other side of the door was muffled and female. "Your fucking meal ticket."

SHADOWED

"Open the door," the woman growled.

Marta turned the deadbolt and slid the chain. When she pulled the door open, she wasn't surprised by who was on the other side. Just disappointed.

Justine Katz didn't wait to be invited in. She brushed past Marta and made herself at home, plopping down on the ratty sofa.

"So, looks like we've got a live one," Justine said.

Marta closed the door and took a seat next to her. "It certainly seems that way."

"What do you mean, 'seems'?" Justine scoffed. "I already told you about the security footage I saw. That kid was hiding shirtless under the stairwell, by himself." She held her hand out, steady. "While he was trying to melt one of his nipples, his other arm had the shirt twisted around his neck. And the whole time, Dustin wasn't moving at all . . . but his shadow *was*. It was having a real good time watching him." She made a jerk-off motion.

"I recall what you explained to me," Marta said. "But I still need to see him a bit more before I can draw my own conclusions. Sometimes, these things are more complicated than they seem."

"I could give a shit if you agree with me or not." Justine stood, seeming to grow more agitated as the conversation extended. "*I'm* the one who spotted the kid and figured out he was being shadowed." She pointed to her chest. "And *I'm* the one who took the kid's lighter and risked my damn career setting that curtain on fire in order to expel him."

"I understand that, but—"

"Quiet! Let me *finish*."

Marta obeyed her command.

"Now . . . I deleted the tape of Dustin under the stairwell, and I made sure the curtain I lit on fire wasn't in an area under surveillance. I created that shitty website that only goes to your profile and sent the kid's mom there. What I'm saying is, I did *everything*. I served them up on a silver fucking platter for you. So it begs the question: If I'm the one who did *all* the legwork, then why the fuck am I sitting here with nothing to show for it?"

"This process doesn't happen overnight," Marta replied calmly. "You know this. We've been through it before."

"Actually, that's an interesting point to bring up. We *have* been through it before, and we've already siphoned what you told me was an extremely dangerous—and as a result, highly valuable—entity. You weren't lying. Kelsey Emit was just looking for a reason to do something heinous; I learned that much watching her in the Extreme Care wing at the school. And there's abso-fucking-lutely no doubt she was a goddamn monster. A monster I created an opportunity for you to capture. And while it was great to help the girl out, hang her picture on the wall, and pat myself on the back, I'm sure you of all people, living in this shithole, know about as well as anyone that you can't live off good vibes alone. So I'm just wondering . . . where's the fucking money from that one?"

"We're talking about black magic and a black market," Marta said. "There is a very specific clientele—who are largely international—and before we started this partnership, the first thing I did was explain that selling *wasn't* going to be a swift process. It comes down to timing and demand in a niche audience where, despite the existence of these entities, believers are scarce."

Justine shook her head. "It's too bad . . . We have such a good thing going. I'm the head of a high-turnover school and have an eye for finding these kids with that . . . *darkness* inside them, and you have the skills to extract it and the connections to sell it. The only problem is, you're not following through on your end of the deal."

Walking around the couch, Justine started to pace.

"For the last extraction, you estimated that such a malignant entity could potentially be sold for a quarter million, maybe more. That's not chump change."

"What are you saying?" Marta asked.

"I guess I just don't trust you." Justine laughed. "Call me crazy, but I haven't seen a dime, so I think I'm allowed to be a little skeptical. You wouldn't have sold *our* darkness by yourself and not told me . . . would you?"

Marta exhaled, gritting her teeth in frustration. Rising from her seat, she approached a small piece of furniture that held several knickknacks.

"Well?" Justine persisted.

Raising an eyebrow, Marta turned back toward Justine. "I can tell you that if I'd sold it already, I wouldn't still be living in this fucking shithole!"

Marta grabbed hold of the small table and flipped it, sending all the junk atop it crashing to the floor. As several figurines broke into pieces, she tried her best to calm her heavy breathing. The fact that she possessed such talent and held items of great worth but remained impoverished infuriated her. The dream of a better life was constantly dangling in front of her, but she just never seemed to be able to grab ahold of it.

Her outburst didn't seem to rattle Justine. With a smirk on her face, she nodded. "Fair enough. But if you have nothing to hide, then you wouldn't mind showing it to me, would you?"

With a sneer of annoyance, Marta led her to the spare room. She opened the door and pointed to a massive cage in the corner of the room.

Justine kept her distance, a look of distress dominating her expression as she laid eyes on the contents of the vast enclosure.

"All right . . . thank you," Justine said, stepping away from the doorway. "You can close it now."

Marta quickly slammed the door, eyes remaining fixed on Justine.

"One last question," Justine said. "I know that thing . . ." She shivered involuntarily. "I know the kid we pulled that out of would've probably been a fucking serial killer if we hadn't. But this boy—Dustin—his darkness doesn't seem as dangerous."

"I told you already, I'll need to spend more time with him before I can be sure about the severity of his situation."

"I'm not asking you to be sure, but based on everything I've already told you, speculate. What's this shadow worth? Ballpark."

Marta thought about it for a moment. "Ballpark, I would say we're looking at maybe fifty to a hundred grand."

"That's it?"

"What did you expect? Based on what I've seen so far and what you've described to me, it's nothing more than a sick pervert. This entity must be some kind of a sexual sadist, a nasty pedophile, or maybe a combination of both. The market doesn't have a high demand for that. Such a timid entity is only so useful."

Justine raised her brow as if trying to judge whether or not Marta was lowballing her on the price.

"Furthermore," Marta continued, "once someone has been shadowed, while their consciousness remains, they're no longer in control of their actions. Instead, they are relegated to spectator—like being in the passenger seat of a car that the shadow drives."

"Why is that even relevant?" Justine asked.

"Because most people in this business are looking for maximum damage. The thing inside of Dustin might cause stress, manipulate people, or even ruin lives. But if transferred, it's not going to be like a bat out of Hell, ripping people to pieces. Whereas a more valuable and lethal darkness, like that one"—Marta pointed at her spare room—"will trigger instant chaos. No methodical plotting. No intellectual preparation at all, really. Just pure horror. *Especially* after lying dormant for so long . . . it will be *starved* for bloodshed."

"So that's what they want most?" Justine asked.

Marta nodded, thinking about the Huxleys' wealth. Regardless of the profit they were set to make from harvesting Dustin's darkness and potentially transmitting it, she knew that the family was ready to bleed more money for her help. She wanted to keep expectations realistic but ensure she didn't turn Justine off while she was taking her time finishing up the gig.

"Now, that's not to say this entity we're targeting can't be sold and still turn us a nice profit. And again, let me remind you—right now this is all just speculation."

"Of course," Justine said smugly, "but I know we've got something. I wouldn't have risked my ass trying to make this happen if I didn't think we'd get a payoff."

"Oh, we'll get a payoff," Marta said with a grin. "Rest assured. I just need you to be patient."

"I've *been* patient."

Shaking her head, Justine approached the front door and tugged it open.

"You might want to consider being a little more proactive," Justine continued. "Maybe if you kept me in the loop, I wouldn't have to show up so out of sorts, concocting worst-case scenarios. But when you're holding an extremely valuable asset that *I* allowed you to attain and weeks go by without hearing a peep . . . what exactly do you expect me to think?"

Marta clenched her fist, not appreciating the tone Justine was taking with her. While she valued their partnership, she wasn't going to be Justine's punching bag.

Still, she knew this wasn't the right time to voice her distress. Marta had been through many struggles in the past—struggles in this very house. But she'd be damned if she was going to allow it to happen again.

"I don't know," she said, shrugging her shoulders. "I'm not a fucking mind reader."

"All I'm asking for is communication. Do yourself a favor and don't make me ask again. Get in touch with whatever third-world shithole or elitist piss-drinker you need to in order to sell that goddamn thing. I want updates, or I'm coming back here, and I won't be this nice next time. Understood?"

Marta gritted her teeth again and forced herself to nod. As she watched Justine slam the door behind her, she knew that wouldn't be the last she saw of her.

MIDNIGHT MESS

"Jesus fucking Christ," Liv whispered.

The dread was already pooling in her stomach when she awoke. At first, she wasn't sure if the sickening sensation in her belly was just a bad feeling or if she needed to use the bathroom. But Liv quickly realized it was the unique breed of instinctual agony that there was no way to predict or understand.

Instead of the calming night and soft glow of the moonlight, a plethora of amber flickers flared outside their bedroom window. The horrifying sight was one she'd need to address right away.

"Bruce!" she shrieked. "Wake up!"

But there wasn't any time to wait around for him. She needed to act immediately.

Liv's yelling instantly snapped Bruce out of his slumber, but it was what continued outside that compelled him out of bed. He watched the memorial tree he'd just planted in front of the house blacken while the smoke billowed up as the flames consumed it. What was supposed to be the lasting memory of Spud was about to be erased before there'd been a chance to appreciate it.

"No . . ." Bruce whispered.

Liv shrieked again, putting on her slippers and reaching for her robe. "We—we've gotta get down there and put that fire out!"

Staring down at the flames, Bruce's eyes locked on to Dustin, who stood before it absentmindedly. Liv hoped he would snap out of it.

"Sweetie, we can't let the house burn down," Liv said.

The flames projected a nightmarish shadow against the trees to the side of the house. The distorted outline was unsettling, spawning internal discomfort. Liv joined Bruce momentarily, watching Dustin.

Slowly, as if he'd somehow sensed they were watching, the boy turned around and looked up at them. His eyes looked black and blank as the flames creepily backlit his bright hair. He didn't look like the boy they'd cradled as a baby. He looked inhuman.

The sound of Bruce's teeth grinding echoed in Liv's eardrums before suddenly stopping.

"I'll fucking kill him," he growled.

INNER DEMONS

The fire might've been put out hours ago, but the rage still burned. Bruce hadn't closed his eyes more than a blink—he was exhausted. The morning sunrise filled him with dread. What hell would the day bring?

"You look like . . ." Liv stopped herself. "Did you get back to sleep?"

Bruce shook his head.

Liv slipped on her blazer. "Maybe you should just take a day off. Marta is gonna be here watching Dustin. It'll help you to get some rest."

"It's my own fault," Bruce mumbled.

"It wasn't *just* you. I could've armed the security system."

"Yeah, but still, he found my fucking lighter again. Even though I changed my hiding spot. Guess it doesn't matter if I don't lock my office."

How could he possibly know? Bruce wondered.

"I guess we just have to lock all the doors in the house from now on too," Liv replied. "We're just lucky he didn't use it inside. As bad as it was . . ." She hesitated. "I guess it could've been worse."

"That's what happens when you get some hope," Bruce grumbled. "You start slipping, get complacent."

Liv slung her purse over her shoulder and approached Bruce in the bed. "It's gonna be okay."

When he felt her body wrap around his, it helped, but her words were still hollow. They were just words people said to each other for comfort. It was a nice gesture, but sadly, it wasn't an honest one, and they both knew it.

Bruce's lower lip quivered. "Poor Spud. He just can't catch a break."

The sight of his agony made her squirm. "Just call out and stay home today, okay? I'll explain what happened to Marta so she's aware." She grabbed the remote from the nightstand and turned the TV on. "Just watch some game shows and pass out."

"Okay," Bruce whispered.

Liv kissed him on the forehead. "All right, I've gotta go. I love you."

"Love you too."

Just before Liv made it to the door, she turned to him. "You do think we should tell her about last night, right?"

"I think we have to," Bruce replied. "How can we expect her to fix this if she doesn't know what's going on?"

"I don't know . . . but she's all we've got left. I just worry about spooking her."

Bruce narrowed his eyes. "Something tells me that she's not the type that scares easy."

BREAKFAST CONVERSATION

Marta set the cup of freshly squeezed orange juice on the table beside Dustin's breakfast. She smiled and pushed it closer to him.

"What's that?" Dustin asked.

"It's orange juice," she replied. "But, it's not just any old juice. This is freshly squeezed. Doesn't taste anything like the bottled stuff. Tastes like candy."

She watched him lift the juice and drink. The expression on his face was what she'd imagined it would be—pleasure and refreshment.

After gulping down close to half of it, his gaze returned to Marta. He grinned with a nastiness in his eyes that never rested. "So, what are we gonna do today?"

Marta returned the smile. "Well, once you finish your breakfast, we can pretty much do whatever you want. I'd like this second day to continue to be mostly about us getting to know each other. Getting comfortable. How does that sound to you?"

Dustin maintained his creepy gawk and guzzled what remained of the orange juice. He shrugged.

"Why does it feel like you already know more than you're letting on?" he asked. "Why does it feel like you're fucking around with me?"

Marta furrowed her brow. Again, she took notice that the boy's vernacular and penchant for cursing was not that of a child in the early teen years but more like the kind of thing an adult might say at a bar.

Dustin's choice of words made her uncomfortable, but as she studied his mannerisms, it was obvious he wasn't going to be a threat much longer.

"You wanna talk about the fire I didn't start?" he asked, slurring his words. "How I *didn't* burn Spud and his stupid fucking tree down? How I—"

Dustin's sentence was cut short as his face planted into the few home fries that remained on his plate.

Marta snatched the cup off the table and brought it to the sink. She used a sponge and liquid soap to wash it out thoroughly, smelling it afterward.

Doesn't smell like anything except clean, she thought.

She walked back to Dustin and picked his limp body up. Marta was grateful that the boy wasn't overweight, but still, carrying him up the stairs wasn't going to be easy. She also would need to be careful not to awaken Bruce.

"Let's go," Marta whispered. "It's almost time."

SICK IN THE HEAD

Despite being exhausted, Bruce couldn't sleep for more than another hour and a half. The gamut of junk food commercials in between the reruns of *Supermarket Sweep* had finally gotten to him.

Damn, I'm hungry, he thought.

The idea that Dustin might be out there infuriated him. The kid was out of his damned mind, and Bruce was starting to feel like he was reaching another breaking point.

Do I . . . do I have something worse inside me than that belt whipping I gave him?

The question scared him, so he decided not to answer it. They'd gone from the whipping in the living room to their meeting with Marta. Despite Dustin burning down Spud's memorial tree the prior night, at least things were sort of trending in a better direction.

Thinking more about his living room conversation with Liv and Marta, he recalled when they'd touched on Dustin's trauma. Bruce found it interesting that Liv had also recently considered the possibility that the incident at her mother's house might've been a tipping point for their son's downward spiral.

That fucking house . . . She bought that creepy-ass house, and then she died.

Bruce unlocked his phone and typed "Scituate Sex Cult Commits Suicide" into the search engine. When the results appeared, he filtered them through the videos tab.

The first video that appeared was the one Bruce selected. It was created by a channel named "All the Gory Details," and after flashing their logo and a warning, the video started to play.

A mash-up of various local and national news reports was spliced together—pieces of different reporters speaking were used to convey the icebreaker message.

"On Tuesday night, a grisly discovery was made as the Scituate Police Department stumbled upon the largest mass suicide the state of Rhode Island has ever seen."

The video switched to a single reporter, a well-dressed man, standing outside of what would eventually become Alice's house. The distinctly yellow crime scene tape was visible in the background.

"The local group of thirteen referred to themselves as 'The Transcenders' because they believed that by partaking in extreme sex acts—including but not limited to autoerotic asphyxiation—they would each be granted the ability to transcend time and space. All members of the group lived under the same roof, in this house behind me, at 78 Wells Street."

The screen transitioned from the reporter to show several photos of members together. They all dressed in similar black clothing and didn't seem to express any emotion. A photo of a longer-haired, hippie-looking man faded to another photo of a woman with a cold stare. Her bald head was shaven down to the skin.

"This wasn't the Scituate PD's first visit to the property. They were called on by the concerned family members of numerous followers for a wellness check. The group's leader, known only as The Mother of Bliss, interacted with authorities on several occasions after being accused of choking a former member of the household unconscious and forcing them to orgasm while they slept."

Jesus fucking Christ, Bruce thought.

A warning flashed on the screen, preparing the viewers for real crime scene photography. Several pictures of the pantless hanging corpses were shown. One of the male corpses still maintained an erection even in death. While these grisly images were displayed, the audio of the news report continued to play.

"The complaint was never officially resolved, but the pressure from local authorities is believed to have egged on members of The Transcenders to complete their 'final release,' as they referred to it. They came together—no pun intended—in a macabre manner. All the bodies were found in the basement, linked and hanging from the same length of circular rope affixed to the ceiling. All but one, that is . . ."

Bruce paused the video, thinking back to when Dustin was in their basement with his own length of rope. There was an eerie resemblance between that situation and the one he was watching unfold in the video.

Bizarre . . .

"The lone member of the group—who is still yet to be identified—that was found upstairs was murdered in a ritualistic fashion. Details are still scarce as the police continue to investigate."

A shudder went down Bruce's spine as he closed the video. He didn't want to think about that night anymore. He'd already had a shitty night and didn't want it to carry into his day.

I'll finish it later. I've watched all I can handle for now.

While Bruce wasn't as hungry after watching the video, he still needed to eat. Setting his phone on the nightstand, he got out of bed.

I should probably check on Marta at some point. Make sure he hasn't scared her off.

When Bruce got into the shower, he noticed his cock had some extra girth. Besides the morning wood, several mock renditions of what Marta might be wearing just a few rooms away popped into his mind. He considered beating off, but in that moment, his hunger outweighed his sexual appetite.

After he dried off and brushed his teeth, Bruce wrapped a towel around his waist. When he opened his dresser, he exhaled with annoyance.

"Damn," he mumbled, looking into the empty drawer that was supposed to contain his underwear.

He glanced at the dirty underwear topping the hamper and considered putting them back on so he could get dressed to go downstairs to the laundry room. He convinced himself that it was gross and defeated the purpose of the shower.

There was another side of him that just wanted to take that walk in nothing but a towel, that *wanted* to be caught in an uncomfortable position. It wasn't like he was going to do anything—Marta was with Dustin anyhow.

Still, the idea of it aroused him enough to go through with it. It was his house, and he needed his underwear.

Fuck it.

BROUGHT TOGETHER

As he stepped out of the room and looked at each end of the hallway, Bruce realized the coast was clear. Quickly creeping down the steps, he wondered how on earth Marta kept the boy so quiet. He hadn't heard a peep out of them all morning.

Bruce rounded the staircase and made his way into the laundry room, then hunched over and looked through the front of the machine. It was just like Liv—she always let clean clothes pile up in the dryer. He reached for the circular door, but before he could pull it open, he heard a voice.

"Bruce, is that you?" Marta asked.

Immediately, his heart exploded, pumping like it was in a competition.

Bruce looked back at her, mouth agape. The casual dress showed off her figure, and in his estimation, the top button appeared to be intentionally undone.

"Where . . . where's Dustin?" Bruce sputtered. It was all he could think to say.

Marta took a step closer and entered the tight laundry space. She leaned up against the washer, intentionally showing her leg.

"Oh, he's fine," she replied. "Asleep right now."

"But it's almost eleven."

"Yeah, well, he had kind of a late night yesterday, from what I heard. Just like you, right?"

She stepped up, closer to him. Bruce kept his fist around the towel, trying to conceal his erection.

"You did too, right?" Marta pressed. "But you don't look tired to me. You look ready."

She reached for the towel and yanked down.

"The fuck are you doing?!" Bruce yelled.

Marta dropped down to her knees and wrapped her fingers around his inflated shaft. "I'm giving you what you want." She slapped his erection as if it was proof of what she was saying and launched a big wad of spit onto the head.

Completely taken aback, Bruce couldn't think. He just watched the spit as it coated his mushroom tip before dribbling down the side.

"You think I don't see how you look at me?" Marta asked. "We have a connection. You can't deny it."

Bruce was shaking with both ecstasy and terror. So many things flashed through his head, but the dominant thought was how damn sexy Marta's eyes were when she looked up at him. So mysterious and exciting. His conscience begged him to pull his hips away from her mouth, but as her wet lips drew closer, he realized it wasn't going to happen.

What about Liv? he thought.

Things had been so insane at the house with Dustin that Bruce hadn't even gotten a chance to follow up on his suspicions. He'd told himself he'd investigate her strange behavior after Spud died, but nothing had come of it.

If she fucked behind my back, then I guess this makes us even.

He'd enforced his thought with enough logic to feel justified in allowing Marta to devour him. Her plump lips parted as his throbbing cock immediately found the back of her throat. He let himself go, grabbing ahold of her hair and pushing himself deeper down inside her neck. Her drool leaked around and all over his shaft.

"Shit . . ." Bruce mumbled. He couldn't remember the last time he'd felt such pleasure.

Marta said nothing, just continued to gag on him. As she exhaled deeply, she unleashed a series of sporadic, wet coughs that forced him to fight off the urge to cum. But as much as Bruce wanted to just blow his load, he couldn't let it be over so soon. He watched the tears trickling down her face as he fucked it and pulled out.

"Oh, baby," she said, gasping for air. "You didn't even get to finish—"

Marta's sentence was cut short by Bruce's eager hand. He lifted her up by her neck and bent her over the washing machine.

"Quiet, bitch," he whispered, pulling up her dress.

The black thong riding up her ass further enticed him. He promptly ripped it off.

"Oh, fuck!" Marta yelled as she felt his tip pushing against her hole. "Just . . . stick it inside me." It was like she wasn't expecting aggression from him but loved every second of it.

As Bruce slid the moist head of his cock around her pussy, he listened to her moans of delight.

"You want it?" he asked, grabbing her hair and pulling her head toward him.

"I need it inside me, please," she begged.

Bruce put his other hand over her lips. "Keep your mouth shut, slut."

The euphoria of her tender lips pressing against his cock was otherworldly. The years of pent-up sexual frustration flooded out. He felt like he'd just traveled to another planet. He lasted longer than he would've expected, pounding away as she nibbled at his fingers. His hips slapped against her ass, and each time he pulled out, his cock got milkier with Marta's runny pleasure.

"Ah, fuck," Bruce moaned.

"Go, blow it inside me, baby," Marta begged. "Fill me up . . . fucking fill me up."

The orgasm was ungodly. It felt like he'd shot a full clip in her cunt. Bruce's legs buckled, and he used Marta's ass to bridge himself up, slumping over on top of her while they both tried to catch their breath.

"Wow . . . that was fun," Marta whispered. "I didn't picture you to be so . . . dominant."

Bruce remained silent, trying his best to soak up the elation. But once the tingling sensation wore off, he quickly cleaned off his cock with the towel.

Marta turned around to face him.

"You're on the pill, right?" he asked.

She took the towel from him and started to wipe the cum out from between her legs.

"Just relax and enjoy the fucking moment," Marta said. "I can tell you haven't in some time."

But as Bruce gorged on the pleasure, other feelings were starting to hit him.

Why did I do this?

He was too bewildered to respond properly. Everything that happened was all still sinking in. The range of thought and emotion was vast.

The fear.

The guilt.

The shame.

The idea that he might've just ruined his life.

At the very, very least, you've severely fucking complicated it.

Bruce had justified fucking Marta by assuming that Liv had done something similar, but now that he'd blown his load and was starting to think clearer, he realized that he'd gone out on a limb. There was a very good chance that what he believed about Liv was completely false.

What the fuck have you done?

"I . . . I've gotta get to work," Bruce stammered.

He didn't really know what else to say. Separating himself from the situation seemed like the most logical decision. He reached into the dryer and quickly yanked out a pair of underwear.

Marta grabbed hold of him before he could move past her. "I said, relax. I'm not gonna tell her anything."

Bruce let out a deep breath. "Thank you."

She relinquished her tight grip on his arm.

"I like you, Bruce. You're just the kind of guy I'm into. That's why I'm going to fix your son. I hope you know that I'd never do anything to jeopardize our relationship."

Relationship . . .? Fuck.

A red flag instantly rose in his mind. He wasn't quite sure how to respond. She'd hit him with a lot all at once.

"Okay . . ." he said. "Good to know. I'm gonna head to work now."

Marta wiped the drool off the side of her face and grinned. "And I'm going to take care of Dustin."

THE SIPHON

Marta stood in Dustin's room, the darkness surrounding her all but for the lone spotlight that shone. After Bruce left for work, she was ready to do some of her own work. She'd angled the light so it projected onto Dustin's motionless body, which she'd positioned in the chair. Beyond the boy, on the floor, sat the bowl littered with strange carvings. The dove with the broken neck lay dead inside.

It's time, she thought.

Looking at the wall where Dustin's shadow projected, she saw her opportunity. A strange outline—not fitting for a young boy. The bulky shadow stretched across the wall, twitching, while Dustin remained still.

Marta approached the bowl cautiously, dropped down to her knees, raised the icepick, and drove it down into the dead dove's spine. She twisted the metal spike inside the creature, causing its blood to leak. As the crimson oozed, she used the bird's carcass to spread the blood around the dish, ensuring that she coated all of the symbols that she'd carved into it.

Once entirely drenched, the magical icons started to glow. Her eyes shifted from the red light to the wall, where the shadow of the bowl projected a darkness that wasn't visible without the shade.

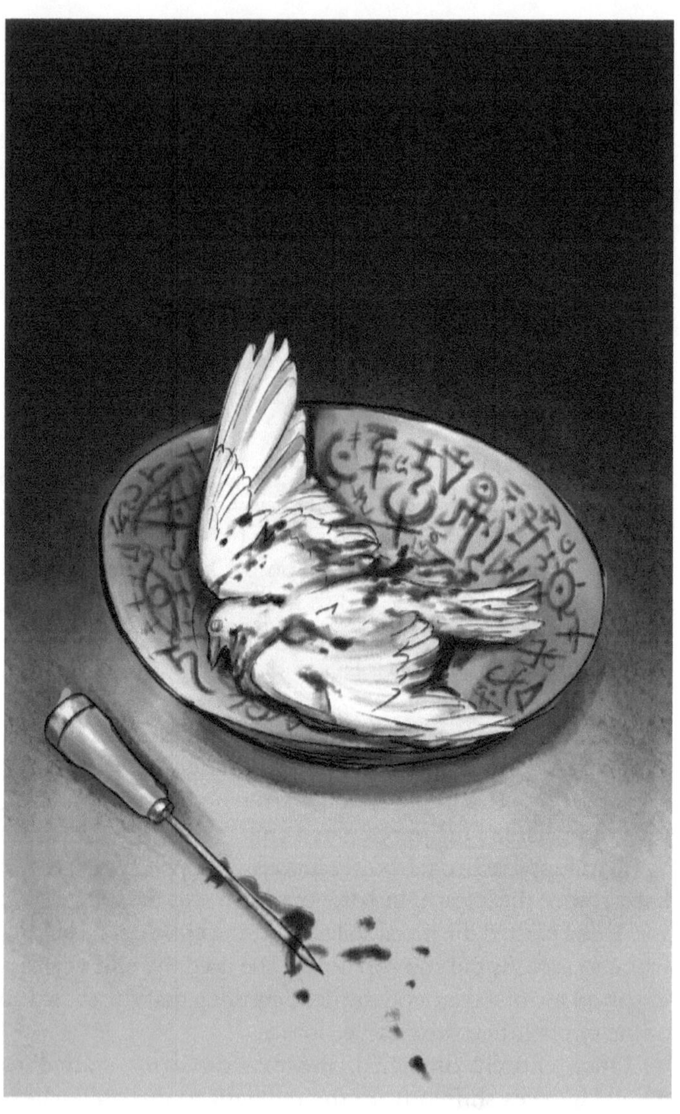

The streams of blackness rose up from the dish, making contact with Dustin's demonic projection. The shadow bent and distorted as it was sucked into the dish like opening a door on a spaceship. The shadow seemed to struggle, fighting against the vacuum effect for several seconds before the entire apparition disappeared all at once.

Marta looked down into the dish at the bloody dove. She watched with a grin as its once white feathers transitioned to the deepest black. Its creamy eyes filled with blood. As its body began to inflate, air filled its lungs again. The bird shrieked in horror, wailing at an ungodly pitch.

The dove shuffled about in the bowl, its broken spine and mangled limbs giving it little range. But Marta knew it would soon be strong again. The hellish birdie still wasn't alive—not quite—but it was now occupied with something truly wicked.

A DIFFERENT PERSON

When Liv entered the house, she was met with something truly shocking. The face Dustin made as he ran at her was a thing of beauty. He was *never* happy to see her, but in that instant, he was ecstatic. Her son had broken through.

Tears dripped down his cheeks—he never cried.

His arms wrapped around her—he never hugged.

Dustin whispered, in the sincerest of sorrows—he never apologized.

"I-I-I didn't ever mean to hurt anyone," he cried. "I wish I could take it back."

Liv rubbed his head and hushed him. "It's okay, baby. I know you didn't. I know you didn't."

"I did so much bad stuff to you and Dad, but that wasn't me . . ." Dustin was now sobbing hysterically. "It wasn't me, I-I swear!"

The sincerity in her son's tone was something Liv was hearing for the first time in a long time. It shook her to the core. Dustin spoke to her with such warmth and compassion in his voice. It was the voice she'd imagined he might have when she had held him in her arms for the first time.

"You believe me, don't you?" Dustin asked.

"I believe you," she whispered, holding him tight.

As Liv stared forward, shaking her head from side to side in disbelief, she saw Marta. The woman stood just a few yards away, smiling.

I was wrong about her, Liv thought. *She's given me my son back. She's given me my* life *back.*

Liv hadn't expected Marta to be able to fix him *ever*, let alone after just a few visits. It was miraculous. It felt more like a magic trick than reality.

Despite the wonderful shift in trajectory, Liv still couldn't help but hold on to her dread. Good things never did seem to last for the Huxleys.

FACING FEAR

Bruce didn't want to go home, but he knew he had to. He could feel himself sweating as he neared the house, heart dropping into his stomach.

What if she's still there? Bruce thought. *What if that entire spiel after she sucked your cock was all just lies and she's already told Liv? What the fuck have you done?!*

Sure, the sex was so hot it was legendary, but he hadn't even taken a minute to enjoy the fresh memory. All day at work and afterward was filled with paranoid questions and worst-case scenarios.

As he steadied the wheel, Bruce reached into his laptop bag and retrieved a pill bottle. He considered breaking one in half.

No, gonna definitely need the whole thing.

It was the only way he'd be able to keep himself from getting too chatty or seeming too antsy. He wasn't prepared for how jarring the dirty decision he'd made would actually be. He was pretty shaken up at the office but thought he'd been masking it well. He'd thought wrong. Several coworkers had asked him if he was all right. He'd lied to the best of his ability, hoping to get some practice in for the lies he'd need to tell Liv later.

This is gonna be brutal.

As Bruce swallowed the pill, he smelled his hand. He'd taken another quick shower before leaving for work but couldn't tell if Marta's scent was still stuck to his fingers.

Hopefully, Liv can't either, or I'm fucking cooked.

"Dammit!" he yelled, slamming his hands against the wheel. He'd traded one moment of pleasure for a lifetime of torture. Nothing about it seemed fair.

A NEW LIFE

Liv's back was to Marta when her eyes connected with Bruce's. It was the first time they'd looked at each other since they'd fucked. It wasn't the same as before. There was restraint now.

There were secrets.

Marta loved secrets. They held power—particularly for a woman. Not that she would need to wield her power unfairly, so long as her new toy did as he was told, when he was told. Along with the restraint in his eyes, she saw fear. That was a good sign. Typically, fear led to obedience. That was all she wanted.

"Are you serious?" Bruce asked, looking into Liv's glossy eyes. "Where is he now?"

"He actually fell asleep," Liv replied, holding Bruce tight. "He was exhausted after having his . . . epiphany. He cried himself to sleep in my arms—didn't want to let go of me. I took him upstairs to rest, but you wouldn't believe it. It's like he's . . ." Liv tried to hold in the tears. "Like he's who we always imagined he'd be."

"That's incredible," Bruce said.

Marta watched Bruce's bittersweet paradigm shift transpire before her eyes. Utter jubilation and regret sixty-nining.

Nothing's free, Bruce, Marta thought. *Not my pussy. Not your son's civility. Nothing.*

"I don't know how she did it," Liv said, grabbing Bruce by the hand. She led him over to where Marta was seated in the kitchen. "But we have Marta to thank."

Bruce pressed his palms together, choosing his words carefully. "This is . . . unbelievable. I can't thank you enough for everything you've done."

"I'm glad I was able to help," Marta replied. "But the real work is just beginning. Something I said in my discussions with Dustin has clicked, but we need to ensure that the progress isn't squandered—that he doesn't regress back into his old ways. But as long as I can continue to have time with him, I'm confident I can keep him on track."

"Of course," Liv said, smiling ear to ear. "We wouldn't have it any other way."

Bruce's leg nervously rocked. "What exactly did you discuss with him?"

"We talked about good and evil," Marta said. "Right and wrong and everything in between. It seems he may have had a convoluted view of morality."

Bruce gave a nervous nod, seeming to quickly regret asking the question.

"But now that he understands what he's done," Marta continued, unleashing a wicked grin, "he's just all eaten up by guilt."

CLOSE YOUR EYES

Dustin lay awake in his bed, holding his arm up. A creepy dream where he'd seen maggots in one of his toys and stared into a mirror only to see the bald woman in the reflection had snapped him out of his slumber.

She's not you anymore, he thought.

It was going to be hard to fall back asleep after looking into her glowing eyes in the dream world, but he felt so tired that he knew it was only a matter of time. Still, there was so much stuff running through his mind. Too many questions. But none more pressing than the one in front of him.

As the moonlight bled in through his window, he gazed upon the wall, and there was clearly something missing. Something that had been weighing him down since he could remember. Something that terrified him.

Where's my *shadow?*

Despite blocking the path of the moonlight, his limb produced no outline. Not only was the thing that had been living inside him gone, but his entire shadow had disappeared.

In a strange way, it comforted him. Often during the last ten years, whenever he saw his shadow, it looked nightmarish. And even worse, whenever he thought about it, a terrible memory seemed to always resurface.

The bodies of the naked men and women thrashing wildly as they hanged, choking while their eyes bulged out of their skulls. Just like his nightmare, he recalled the feeling of helplessness the moment he'd gazed into the bald woman's eyes. The sheer weight of her darkness had emotionally and physically restrained him.

He'd sat by for far too long, watching his life be made into something sinister. Much of it was a blur. It didn't feel real—more like watching a horrible television show for a decade straight.

Still, it was something Dustin had grown to accept. His consciousness was suppressed enough that he imagined it would be like that forever.

Until today.

He hadn't gotten much time to think during all his developmental years. So much time had been wasted while he just sat by idly and watched. It was like he was still there but didn't have a say in anything. He knew what was happening was horrible and wrong, but that didn't matter.

Until now. Dustin was finally unshackled; the mountainous strain had been lifted by that strange woman and his sins had come tumbling down.

If she was trying to help me, why didn't she show Mom and Dad that picture of Spud?

There were some things about Marta that he still couldn't make sense of. And thinking about the dog made him sad. He missed him dearly.

I never wanted to kill Spud, or hurt Jimmy, or start fires.

Maybe the worst part was the way his parents had looked at him for so long. Their eyes filled with disappointment, depression, and even what he believed to be hatred. These were looks that he'd had to endure every single day. He should've been in control of it, but he wasn't.

The feeling was unbearable. He didn't know what had happened to bring him to that place in time, but it almost didn't even matter—he was just grateful to arrive. He would make the best out of it.

Dustin would find a way to make his parents forget about the past. To make them proud of the lost cause they'd believed him to be. He felt like, for almost his entire life, he hadn't been himself. Like he was just finally getting to understand who he was and maybe even what he wanted. But it was hard to focus. All he could do was think about the awful memories the bald woman—The Mother of Bliss, as she'd referred to herself—had created.

When Dustin closed his eyelids, they were wet. He knew, even though they provided darkness, that darkness wouldn't allow him freedom.

There was no escape from the past.

CONNECTED AGAIN

As Bruce pulled his throbbing rod out of Liv, it was obvious that evening was a night of celebration. They hadn't fucked like that since before they'd had Dustin. The orgasm felt heavenly, but it was spoiled by his guilt. He'd cheated her out of what was supposed to be a metamorphosis moment for the two of them.

"Goddamn . . . that was something else," Liv said, rubbing herself. "I came twice." She exhaled, rubbing her thighs together.

Things were suddenly so passionate again. Liv had pounced on him when they'd gotten into the bedroom. It was like knowing her child had been restored gave her back her confidence.

Bruce had been in his twenties the last time he'd had his cock inside two women in the same twenty-four-hour period. It was fine then, but was not a milestone he'd intended on revisiting after finding the love of his life.

A moment of silence passed. He didn't know what to say, but finally, he opened his mouth and the words just came out.

"I fucking love you."

She turned to cuddle him, laying her head on his chest.

"I love you too, sweetie."

He remained disappointed in himself but didn't want to sully the moment for her. Forcing himself to move on, he kissed her on the top of the head.

"So what made you decide to go to work?" Liv asked. "After last night, I don't even know how you were able to function."

Bruce's heartbeat ramped up. Thankfully, he'd just finished fucking her, so it probably didn't seem too odd. But her ear was just about directly on his chest, so he wondered if she picked up on the slight increase in pace.

"I slept until about lunchtime. Felt pretty good about it. And honestly, after what Dustin did, I just thought it might be best to keep some space between us. I wasn't going to do anything to him, but I just didn't want to get in the way of his therapy."

Fuck, was that answer too long? Bruce thought. *Did I sound too nervous? Stupid! Why the hell couldn't you just give a simple answer to her?!*

She let out a deep breath—not one of satisfaction but of obvious worry.

Bruce's heartbeat pumped madly, accelerating even more. "What's wrong?"

"I just can't get over it," she replied.

"I know . . . I don't think you're lying"—he couldn't believe *he'd* just said that to *her*—"but without seeing him myself, it's hard not to be skeptical."

"I don't blame you. If it would've been you trying to explain it to me, I don't think I'd have believed it either. But even still, I just got this feeling . . . like . . ." She sighed and groaned.

It was clear she didn't want to say it. Neither did Bruce. Still, he asked out of courtesy. It was the least he could do for the woman he'd just betrayed.

"Like what?"

"Like something's terribly wrong. Like at any minute, all of this is just going to unravel and it'll be like nothing ever changed in the first place."

The words she shared had dual meaning to him—they could be applied to the situation with Dustin or with Marta.

"It's gonna be okay, I promise," he lied. "I mean, he hugged you today, right? He fucking *hugged* you." Bruce looked at the ceiling, still blown away by the revelation.

"You're right, babe," Liv said, rubbing his chest, then flipping over on her other side. "I'm sure I'll get over it."

The word choice had so much irony attached to it. Bruce knew it was possible she might get over it. But if she found out about Marta, everything would come crashing down in an instant.

"Goodnight, I love you," Liv said.

"I love you too, babe."

As a few moments passed, Bruce realized he couldn't sleep. The guilt and complexity of the situation weighed heavily on his soul. He looked at his nightstand, hoping his phone might be able to distract him from his restlessness.

Plugging in his earbuds, he looked at the screen and unlocked it. When he clicked on the browser, he was confronted by the same video clip about the mass suicide he'd been watching earlier that day. While it wasn't exactly the most cheerful content, Bruce pressed play, his curiosity getting the best of him.

COLD FEET

The Mother of Bliss sat in her chair listening to the series of loud pops rattle off in succession. With each knuckle that cracked, her pussy got wetter. She watched Ze as he stood shirtless, enticing her with his extra-long fingers.

Ropes and clothing had their own distinct textures, and while she didn't hate how they felt around her throat, she much preferred a human touch. Ze's hands were godly. The way they wrapped around her entire neck when he cut off her air supply gave her a feeling that no object or other person could. She adored him so much that she'd given him his name. Ze was the pet name that only she used to show him affection. But to the rest of the group, he was Squeeze.

"I wish you would reconsider," she said. "I want you to be by my side—I want us to be there together."

"I want it too," Ze said, wrapping his fingers around her throat. "But it's just not me . . . I'm the one who does the choking, not the one who gets choked."

The tall man was a gentle giant. As he applied soft pressure to her throat, The Mother of Bliss let out a moan of pleasure, reaching up under her dress and rubbing her clit.

"I-I'm scared . . . I don't wanna transcend," he continued, squeezing tighter. "I just don't think it's right for me, Momma."

She liked it when he called her Momma while choking her. Even though Ze was just a man who had come to her house looking for guidance, he wasn't like all the others who had joined her mission. They'd developed a unique bond. The others called her Mother, but not Ze. They had a special connection.

As his long fingers tightened with the perfect pressure, she rode the wave, ascending to a climax. She felt her eyes rise out of their sockets ever so slightly.

When she came down from the high, it took her a minute to think straight again. As Ze let go of her, she extracted her hand and toyed with the gooey pile of cream that sat in her palm.

"It's a shame that you won't join by choice," she said, looking at the thick discharge in her hand.

Ze furrowed his brow, seemingly confused by her wording. When she reached under the cushion of the recliner and extracted the knife, she could see his panic setting in.

"Hold him down," The Mother of Bliss commanded.

Before Ze could react, several members of the group rushed into the room. The obedient bald-headed men and women forced Ze to his knees after taking control of his arms.

"W-what's happening?" Ze cried.

The Mother of Bliss carefully took the blade into her hand, sliding her pleasure sludge all over the shaft of the steel.

"I gave you so much free will," she said. "I made exceptions for you—exceptions that no one else got. I let you keep your hair..." She rubbed her hand over her hairless head with an ashamed look on her face. "I let you do the choking, when everyone knows we *all* choke . . . and do you know why?"

"I-I'm sorry, Momma!" Ze pleaded, tears starting to run down his face. "I don't know what I did to upset—"

"I said, do you know why?!"

He shook his head.

"Because you're special to me," she whispered. "You're a very sweet and often confused young man. But when you came into my life, you brightened it. You're my Squeeze. But when you got cold feet, when you told me that you weren't going to transcend with us—with me!—you . . . you broke my heart."

She raised the runny blade and angled it down at Ze's heart. A rope of her white secretion dripped from the tip of the knife and landed on his face.

"Momma, please, no!"

She shook her head. "Momma knows best."

The wet blade plunged into Ze's chest, causing him to emit a horrible shriek. As much as it pained The Mother of Bliss to hear her sweet Ze's painful wails and pleas, she knew she'd done right.

Blood surged out of the wound as she used a sawing motion to drive the blade down to his gut. With crimson oozing from his mouth, she yanked the blade out of the gaping hole in his chest. She considered stopping, but the idea of Ze not being by her side was too much to bear. She drove the knife into his torso countless times over before finally extracting it and letting him fall to his side.

Pointing the gory steel at his motionless body, she commanded her followers. "Transcenders! Let this be an example to *everyone*! There is no going back! We will transcend together! And as you know, we leave no one behind . . ."

"Together," they all replied in chorus.

Ze remained on the floor, gurgling on his own blood, the gaping hole in his chest surrounded by a peppering of smaller puncture wounds.

She returned her gaze to her followers. "Plant the seed where he bleeds." Her eyes darted to the gory hole in Ze's chest. "And he shall join us again once we transcend."

"Yes, Mother," they all replied in chorus again.

The followers immediately removed their robes and stood over him, naked. As The Mother of Bliss looked on, The Transcenders began to pleasure themselves, the men stroking their shafts, the women fingering their holes and rubbing their clits.

Since Ze wouldn't come along willingly, The Mother of Bliss knew the ritual sacrifice was her only other option. Coating the blade in her own fluid and harnessing her vigor and that of all her followers was the only way.

"Go there for him!" she yelled. "Raise his spirit!"

As the moaning followers howled with pleasure, one by one, they started to pop. Cumshots and squirting fits exploded, some simultaneous and others in close succession. Some of the women wiped the creamy pleasure juice coating their hands inside their fallen disciple by fingering his wounds. The gunky rain showered Ze as he took his final breaths, painting his body and the glistening wounds upon it.

***

When Dustin awoke this time, he was screaming, but nothing was coming out of his mouth. He slowly realized that it was just a nightmare—that the evil bald woman was no longer in control of his body.

As he calmed himself, Dustin recalled the countless daydreams and nightmares he'd had while infected with her wicked presence. Through these dreams and her memories, he'd gotten to know her disturbed followers and their warped ways. He'd relived The Mother of Bliss's fantasies, Ze's murder, and the mass suicide of The Transcenders countless times. In that moment, Dustin knew that it was time to move on.

It's just a dream, he thought.

The idea of continuing to deal with these nightmares—being harassed by the psychological scars she'd left him with—made him worry. But if the dreams were all he had to deal with in order to move on from the ten-year prison sentence he'd served, then so be it.

She can have my dreams. I just want my life.

As Dustin closed his eyes again, he took a deep breath. Those horrible times had galvanized him, had made him strong enough to push past the darkness once and for all.

It's just a dream. It's just a dream . . .

A WANDERING MIND

Liv was having trouble sleeping, but it wasn't the normal trouble. Instead of nightmares, she'd woken up hours into her slumber filled with excitement. She wanted to rush into Dustin's room, hug him, and then tell him how much she loved him. The entire situation felt so alien, like she was lying to herself, but she knew she wasn't.

Hours earlier, Liv's ear had rested on Bruce's chest, listening to it pound. Her own heart had pounded even harder. Part of it was the fucking, but there were other reasons too. She had her husband back. And even more than her husband, Liv had her family back.

So stupid, Liv thought. *You waited this long already . . . Why couldn't you just be patient? It was all right there in front of you.*

It was depressing that their special moment, when they finally rekindled their spark, had to be tarnished. As Liv lay quietly, all she could think about was Fred. How she'd gone, so long, fighting for Bruce, fighting for her family, only to give in. One afternoon of selfishness could spoil it all.

It'll be okay. I've . . . I've just got to let him know that it's over. No more racy texts, no nothing. Eventually, I'll find a way to tell

Bruce. I'll do whatever it takes to make things right between us again. Whatever *it takes.*

The lone hookup with Fred would be an anomaly—a dark secret that she would take to the grave. After close to a decade of living in constant turmoil, there was no way she was going to rock the boat right after the waters had finally settled. She would find a way to deal with the guilt. If she had to continue to binge eat to dull the pain, so be it. One way or another, she would move on until there was enough separation from the affair to break it to him.

She turned to Bruce, who was sleeping, and gently nudged him. "Bruce?"

It took a few tries, but he came awake.

"Hey," he whispered.

"I can't wait for you to spend time with him," Liv said. "He really is different—I mean it."

Bruce let his fingers stroke her arm lovingly. "I believe you . . . I can't wait either."

Liv's internal decision still couldn't help her shake the horrible feeling inside. But seeing that she and Bruce were on a new wavelength, maybe helping him feel better would help her too.

Sliding her head down his abdomen, she grabbed hold of his cock.

Bruce moaned with pleasure.

"You know what else I can't wait for?" Liv asked, biting her lip and squeezing his dick until it solidified again.

Make him feel good and you'll feel good too.

CAST ASIDE

Bruce scrubbed his body, but after what he'd done, he knew he'd never truly be clean again. He wondered if the prior night was Liv's instincts or something else.

There was no way for her to know what happened, he thought. *She wouldn't have fucked you if that was the case.*

She'd seemed normal enough this morning, had even suggested that he take the day off from work and be with Dustin to experience his transformation firsthand. As much as he would've liked to, Bruce knew it was best for him not to be at the house again when Marta was there and Liv wasn't. He'd fed her some bullshit excuse about work.

There was a side of him that was filled with temptation. He'd fucked them both within a very tight window. Marta was like a madwoman. He could tell she liked it rough. There was this sluttiness about her when she fucked that was incredibly hot. Like she just wanted him to treat her like a whore. Before he realized what was happening, Bruce looked down at his hard cock in his sudsy hand.

That's a terrible idea!

He pushed his erection away and started to rinse off. But just as he did, there was a tap on the shower door. His heart pounded with mighty thuds of terror.

"Honey, I'm about to leave for work," Liv said.

Bruce exhaled in relief.

She slid the frosted door partially open and kissed him on the lips. "I put your phone on the sink. It dinged. I don't know if it was that thing at the office you were talking about, but I've gotta run." She went to close the shower door but stopped herself. "Listen . . . I know that Dustin having this change of heart doesn't make up for everything he's done. I know you're probably still hurt. But if he's awake when you leave, just talk to him. I know you'll see what I mean."

"Okay, sweetie," Bruce said. "I love you and hope you have a great day."

"I love you too," she said, turning on the air vent in the bathroom upon her exit.

He finished up in the shower and dried off, all the while still wondering who would be sending him a message so early in the day. Once his hands were dry, he grabbed the phone from the sink and unlocked it. The name that popped up wasn't one that he'd hoped to see.

Before you leave, we need to talk, Marta's message read.

"Fuck," he said.

"I'd love to," Marta replied.

Bruce snapped his head up. She lay just outside the doorway of the bathroom. Marta curled back on the bed seductively, rubbing her arms and arching her back.

"But this time, I want you to fuck me in your bed," she confessed.

"What—are you crazy?! You can't be in here!" Bruce yelled.

"Of course I can."

"You're supposed to be watching Dustin."

"After he had his orange juice, he fell asleep upstairs. It'll be just like before—he won't hear a thing."

Bruce closed the door and locked it. Thankfully, he'd set his clothes on the counter already. He quickly slipped into them, forcing himself to get dressed before approaching Marta.

"What are you doing?" she asked through the door.

"I'm getting ready for work," Bruce replied.

"But you can't fuck me with your clothes on."

Bruce huffed under his breath. "I'm not fucking you again, Marta. That was a mistake. It's over and—and the both of us have to move on, okay?"

There was no answer.

"I promise I wasn't trying to be a scumbag. We've just—Liv and I have had some issues, and I did something that I shouldn't have. But I still love my wife. You're an amazing and beautiful woman—we just met under the wrong set of circumstances. I'm sorry."

Bruce zipped up his fly and buttoned his pants while awaiting the answer. When none came, he said again, "I'm sorry, Marta. Okay?"

"That's what I needed to hear," she replied.

As Bruce finished buttoning his shirt, he reached for the doorhandle. But by the time he pulled it open, Marta was no longer on the other side.

Bruce rushed downstairs. In a matter of minutes, he'd gathered everything he needed to get to work and away from Marta. But as he opened the front door, he was stopped by an alarming sight.

A tall, burly man's wide fist flew toward his face, blasting him square between the eyes. Dazed, Bruce tumbled onto the floor, desperately trying to get his bearings. As he looked up, his vision started to clear, and he focused on a face that he didn't recognize.

"Who the—?"

Bruce's words were promptly cut off by the man's shouting. "My boy hasn't spoken a word—hasn't even opened his mouth since he stayed at this goddamn house!"

Suddenly, Bruce realized who the man was. Liv had told him how upset Jimmy Stevens's father, Russell, had been. They hadn't heard from him since the incident. He'd probably been stewing the entire time, just thinking about what he was going to say and how he was going to say it.

"I've gotta pry his mouth open every night," Russell said, growing more and more upset, "and listen to him fucking cry while I force-feed him."

Bruce remained on the ground, still stunned by the attack, scrambling to find his words.

"That . . . I'm sorry," Bruce said. "I wish it didn't—"

"Save the apologies! I came here to tell you one thing. You better fucking pray my son gets better soon. Because if he doesn't . . . then there's gonna be hell to pay."

Russell leaned over Bruce and spit in his face before turning his back and heading for his truck.

As Bruce wiped the spit off his cheek, Marta appeared. She stood in the doorway with her phone out, aiming it at the truck as it drove away.

"What are you doing?" Bruce asked.

Marta put the phone in her pocket and made her way back to the staircase. "You'll find out soon enough."

END OF THE AFFAIR

When Fred pulled Liv into the closet, she didn't expect him to try and stick his tongue down her throat. Sure, he'd texted her such office fantasies, but to actually try it seemed utterly absurd.

"What the hell are you doing?" Liv asked as the door closed.

Fred continued to try kissing her while groping until Liv pushed him off.

"Stop it!" she yelled.

A snarl of discontent scrunched Fred's face.

"What the fuck is your problem? You don't answer my texts for days, act like I don't even exist, and now *you're* giving *me* attitude?"

Since he seemed angry, Liv thought she might try a calm approach. She hoped that would be the easiest way for her to back out of the entire situation.

"Listen," she said. "I'm sorry I didn't get back to you . . . I've had a lot going on. But either way, it's probably for the best. I'm not going to be able to continue this."

Confusion swirled on Fred's face. "Continue what?"

"You and me. We can't see each other anymore."

He laughed. "You're kidding, right?"

Eyes widening, Liv felt a surge of frustration pushing to the surface.

"What the hell did you expect?" she asked.

Fred took a step closer to her, coming face-to-face. He looked down on her in a domineering manner.

"What did I expect?" he asked. "I expected a fat pig like you to wait at my beck and call. I did you a favor fucking your sloppy ass, and now you wanna cut me off? No, you don't quit me, bitch. *I* tell you when this is done."

Taken aback by his hurtful remarks and anger, Liv struggled to find words. But she knew she couldn't just back down. It had to end.

"Are you out of your mind?" she asked. "Just because we had sex one time doesn't mean I'm your property."

"No!" Fred punched the filing cabinet, making her jump. "That's where you're wrong." His psychotic eyes suddenly lost their intensity as he grinned. "Hey, I'm not asking for the world. But I'll tell you exactly how this is gonna play out. You're gonna fuck me whenever I'm feeling lazy. You know, when I don't feel like putting in effort to pull a girl who's actually attractive. I like to have a cum dumpster like you on standby."

If Liv wasn't so terrified by his anger, she might've been even more hurt by the nasty insults he laced his rant with.

"Now listen, I know you have a family. I'm not going to go all crazy and fuck you every night. But I'm gonna need that pussy at least once or twice a week. I'm willing to play nice if you are. I don't wanna ruin your life or anything . . . but I will. If I have to."

Fred pulled out his phone and showed her a video. It was of Liv. She stood naked in his bathroom, attempting to clean the cum off her back with a towel.

"There's a real nice shower scene after that too," he said. "It'd be a shame if limp-dick Bruce gets ahold of this. I wonder what he'd think."

"You're fucking sick," Liv said, sniffing.

"I could screenshot you naked and print out close-up images, maybe mail them to ol' Bruce one by one—you know, treat it like a puzzle and let him put it together over time. Yeah, that sounds like fun." The grin melted off Fred's face. "But if you'd rather I didn't, then why don't you get on your goddamn knees right now."

Liv was shaking with rage, she was so upset. She wanted to cry, but the blazing fury inside her was too powerful. Falling to her knees, she grabbed onto his belt buckle and looked up at Fred.

"Is this what you want?" she asked.

"You know *exactly* what I fucking want, bitch," Fred replied.

Cocking her arm back, Liv launched her fist forward. Her knuckles and wedding ring connected with his balls and dick, sending him to the ground with a groan.

Rushing to her feet, Liv reached for the door handle and looked back.

"Get on *your* fucking knees, asshole," she said.

Yanking the door open, Liv ran out and didn't look back.

UNSETTLED

The cartoon on the screen was funny, but not enough to keep Bruce's attention. He was lost inside his head for many different reasons. He wasn't sure if it was the drugs or just life, but the brain fog had hit him full-force at work, and it seemed to follow him home.

Marta was still on his mind. Thankfully, she was gone when he got home.

Maybe she finally got the hint? Bruce wondered.

If not, he was going to be pulling a tightrope act every day. Either way, he would still feel like shit inside.

Won't I?

He was starting to question it. Each time he swallowed an extra pill, he got a wavy sensation. It made him feel like maybe the offense wasn't as bad as he was making it out to be. It was an internal argument that he was constantly going back and forth with.

Dustin squeezed his hand, pulling his focus away from the Marta situation.

"Dad, I—I just wanted to say sorry again," Dustin confessed.

"It's okay. I forgive you," Bruce replied, patting his leg several times to comfort him.

Dustin's latest apology made Bruce feel like a terrible father. He should've been over the moon that his son was back. But instead, he was worrying about how a selfish choice he'd made could potentially break apart a family that had, against all odds, finally been glued back together.

Bruce wasn't any less shocked by his son's actions than when he'd arrived home. The boy had shown true remorse, begging both him and Liv for understanding every few minutes, clearly unable to believe they actually forgave him in the first place. The tearful apology was beyond moving—no matter how many times he repeated it. It was unbelievable. They were all sitting together like a family on the couch—just a trio of normal people.

"You don't have to feel guilty or keep apologizing," Bruce continued.

"You . . . you promise?" Dustin asked.

"I promise."

Liv looked on with such adoration. Like she never imagined such a situation could unfold. Based on how things had been for years, it would've been more likely that one of them finally snapped and killed the other than all of them coming together.

"Hey, Dad," Dustin said.

Bruce looked at him.

"Would you come upstairs with me for a second?"

When Bruce shifted his gaze to Liv for approval, she was already nodding.

"Sure thing, bud," Bruce said.

As Dustin scampered up the stairs, Bruce followed. When they reached his room, Dustin closed the door.

"So, what's up?" Bruce asked.

Dustin moved to the corner of his room and took hold of the hockey stick.

"Do you . . . you think I could sign up for hockey?"

If the pills weren't numbing Bruce so profoundly, he probably would've cried. Memories of the young and curious son he loved came back to him. All he'd ever wanted was to guide his boy and watch him do the things most every boy loved to do.

Dustin's back. He really is back.

"Of course . . . Son."

It took him a moment to get the word out. He hadn't called him that in some time. But Dustin was his son, and for the first time in a long time, he was grateful for that.

"I wanna try wrestling too," Dustin continued. "You know, just like you did in college." His lip started to quiver. "I always wanted to be just like you, Dad. Even when I was all messed up."

Bruce got a tickle in his nose—the power and heart fueling their conversation outweighed the drugs.

"I-I just want you to know, that was always w-w-what I wanted," Dustin said through the tears.

Bruce pulled him in for a hug and squeezed extra tight. There was nothing that needed to be said, and he knew showing Dustin his love would mean so much more. When Dustin cried into his chest, it felt like a cry that had been building up inside the boy for ages was finally released—like floodgates to a dam that had finally broken.

For a brief moment, the thought of asking Dustin what changed crossed his mind. He'd discussed that very topic with Liv earlier—if they should even ask about why Dustin was the way he was for so long. They'd decided it was too soon to stir up those old demons. There was no telling if such thoughts might lead to Dustin relapsing into his old ways. It was best to let Marta—the trained professional—keep working her magic until they were further removed from the wicked streak of calamity.

"I know, Son," Bruce whispered as Dustin's cries finally started to simmer down. "We can do whatever you want, okay?"

"O-okay, Dad."

Staring at his red face as he wiped the tears away sullied Bruces heart with more gloom. He didn't want his boy to keep feeling terrible.

"I don't want you to be sad," Bruce said. "You know it's okay to smile, right?"

Dustin cracked a half grin and nodded.

"Trust me," Bruce said, "once you start getting into hockey and especially wrestling, you're gonna be having so much fun you're not gonna be able to stop smiling."

"Sounds awesome," Dustin said.

"Now what do you say we head back downstairs? We can talk more about it and see if your mother is willing to fix us something to eat, okay?"

Dustin grinned wider. "Okay."

They raced down the stairs excitedly until they reached the living room.

"Guess what?" Bruce asked.

"What?" Liv asked, looking at them like she couldn't be happier.

"Dustin wants to sign up for hockey *and* wrestling."

As much as Bruce could see Liv was struggling to hold it together, she did her best not to spoil the moment by crying. But he could see how proud she was.

"That's . . . incredible," she whispered.

"But there's a few things I can show him at the house before he even signs up. He'll be going in there with a little advantage."

Bruce jokingly grabbed Dustin and wrestled with him on the couch. He gently slipped in a full nelson wrestling hold but let Dustin out of it almost immediately. They continued to playfully scuffle. Dustin giggled with glee.

"You two are just perfect," Liv said, rubbing Dustin's head. "This . . . is perfect."

She's right.

But Bruce knew that such perfection could easily be flushed down the toilet. Oddly enough, it was the same person who was the catalyst for their perfect world that could potentially be the one to destroy it.

A DEEPER DARKNESS

In her dilapidated house, Marta stood looking into the mirror. Her face was on par with that of a runway model, but that didn't seem to matter.

You're never good enough for anyone who matters, she thought. *Never fucking good enough! But Liv is? How can that fat, ugly bitch be but not me?!*

Marta grimaced and ground her teeth. She thought about Liv's many warts that were plainly visible right on the surface. From her lack of confidence to her stupid freckles, those flabby love handles, and even her physical and mental softness—it was all pathetic.

"Why would he even want her?!" Marta bellowed, swinging her fist into the mirror. The powerful blow fractured the glass into reflective pieces and sent them crashing down at her feet.

Breathing heavily, Marta stepped away from the shards and sat on the couch. With her hands on her head, she tried to calm herself, but her train of thought was interrupted by a pounding on the door. She glared at the entrance, not sure how to feel. The pounding continued, causing her to jump from the sofa and storm toward the door.

In a flash, she'd turned the lock and yanked the handle. Standing on the other side was exactly who she'd expected—the only person who visited her these days.

"How hard is it to just follow up with me?!" Justine yelled. "Last time I was here I told you that—"

Marta wrapped her hands around Justine's neck and started to squeeze. Dragging her inside, she tossed Justine into the shattered mirror. After locking the door, Marta was already lifting Justine up from the pile of shards. The slices on her arms and legs bled as Marta led her toward the spare room.

"Wait!" Justine cried. "I-I didn't mean it that way! What are you do—?"

Justine's speech was stunted again as Marta smashed her face into the wooden door. Nose oozing blood and snot, she fell to the ground while Marta turned the handle.

The commotion of screaming and fighting had caused an uproar. Marta turned toward the birds that were absolutely losing their minds inside the gigantic cage.

The pair of demonic doves were malformed. The bird she'd used as the vehicle for Dustin's shadow still remained black as the night and with eyes that were blood red. While that bird was impressively frightening, the one it shared the cage with was in a league of its own.

The mammoth dove that Justine had arranged to take on Kelsey Emit's demons held the darkness of a dozen murderers. It harbored all the same evil traits as the smaller dove, in addition to vile areas of advanced necrosis. The slimy patches of defeathered flesh housed maggots, worms, and other fattened insects.

Overflowing with insidiousness, the creature was closer to the size of an adult goose rather than a dove. Like the others, it moved awkwardly because of its broken neck and mangled limbs, but the blood and gore that caked its sharp beak made it obvious that it could still do some damage.

There was no better evidence of this than the corpse of the destroyed man on the ground.

Massive piles of black and white bird shit littered the floor around the man who had dared to threaten her love. The man who might've been responsible for ruining her meal ticket had she not hunted him down and seduced him. The drink Marta had given him kept him asleep while the doves did most of their dining.

In just about an hour's time, they'd eaten Russell's eyes, fingers, and face. And when he'd awoke in the cage, blinded and bloody and screaming, to a frenzy of pecks from the sinister birds, he was already so wounded that he had little chance of making it. He was only conscious for a short time before the twisted birds had pecked open his throat, creating a fountain of blood that would eventually lead to his death.

The giant blood-soaked dove gyrated with madness and fury as its eyes found Justine.

"You see that?" Marta said. "Just like I told you, a real killer! One way or another, he's going to make us—well, I mean *me*—a lot of money."

Marta pulled the cage door open and immediately kicked Justine's dazed body into harm's way. It only took seconds for the birds to pounce.

"Marta! Marta!" Justine squealed as a sharp, blackened beak stabbed through the side of her cheek and scraped against her tooth. "Ahhhhhhhhhhhhhh! Please, I'm sorry! Please—"

As she tried to apologize, the smaller of the dark doves shoved its head into her mouth, using its body to obstruct her airway. As she choked and gagged on the girth of the dove, tears streaked down Justine's face and blood oozed from her mouth.

The larger dove's pointed beak pierced through her eyeball with ease, pulling the pupil apart like it was taking the skin off a grape.

Still unable to breathe, Justine fell backward. As she gagged on the dove in her mouth, the bigger bird continued to peck and scrape the flesh off her while her body quaked in agony.

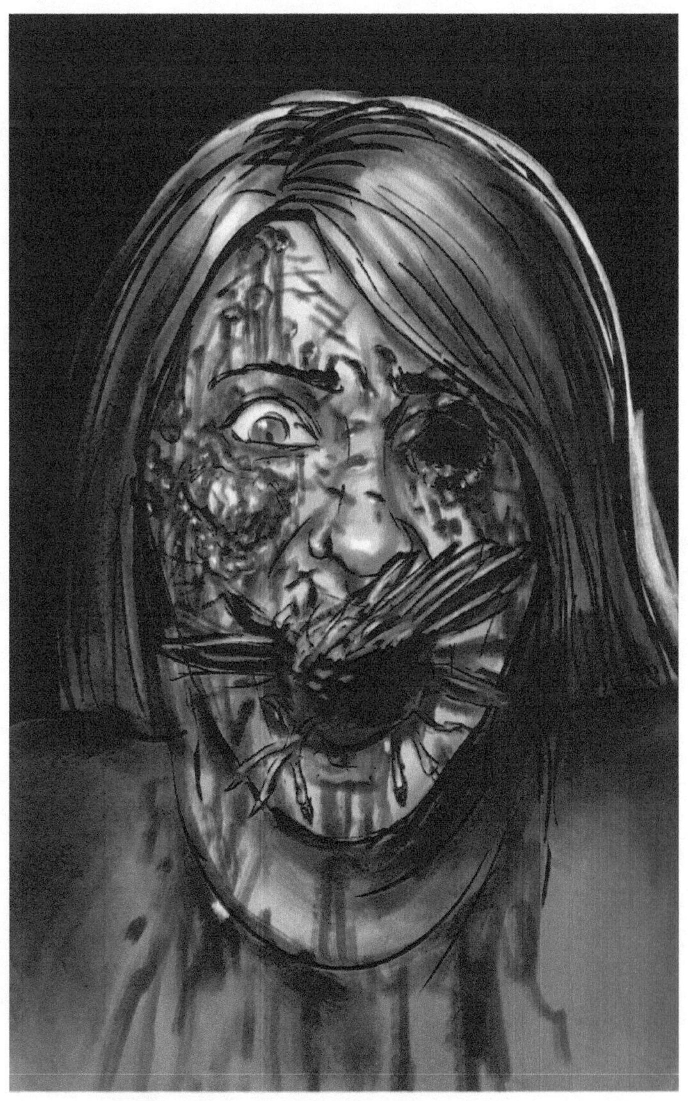

"It's time I got what I deserve," Marta said. "I'm not going to let myself die in this fucking shack."

The massive bird continued to use its beak to strike Justine's face repeatedly. The blows were so furious that the creature had already uncovered her cheekbone.

"And no one"—Marta pointed at Justine and then Russell—"not you, that bastard, or that ginger cunt, is going to stop me from finally getting what's mine."

Marta smiled as she listened to Justine's death rattle. That wasn't the first one she'd heard, and she didn't plan on it being the last.

THE MESSAGE

Bruce had just finished settling in when he got the message. Each time Marta's name popped up on his phone, his heart sank. The small audio clip came along with the text *Come home now.* He had no choice but to play the clip.

The recording was a little muffled, but the words were clear enough. It was his own voice.

"I'm not fucking you again, Marta. That was a mistake. It's over and—and the both of us have to move on, okay? . . . I promise I wasn't trying to be a scumbag."

"Fuck, fuck, fuck!" Bruce said, pounding his hand on his desk harder each time he cursed.

He immediately went for his crutch and cracked open the bottle of pills. As he washed one down with his coffee, he only grew more upset. The terror in his belly was more profound than ever.

For the first time in a long time, he had something to lose. His family was relatively normal again, and for that much, he had to be grateful. But ironically, the woman who'd given him his life back was now the one threatening to unravel it.

Can't make this shit up, Bruce thought. *That bitch is crazy. I knew she was up to something. It was just a matter of time.*

There was no way around it. Marta had him by the balls. It was a feeling he wasn't accustomed to with anyone outside of Dustin. Because his son had acted out so much over the years, Bruce had made it a point not to allow anyone else in his life to manipulate him in the slightest.

But things had changed. That standard was no more.

As Bruce reached for his laptop bag, his heart felt like it was going to explode. He tried his best to ignore the horrible sensation and headed for the door.

OFFICE AWKWARDNESS

Just keep your head down, Liv thought. *If you act like nothing happened, then it'll be like nothing happened.*

From her peripheral, Liv attempted to spot Fred. She could feel his eyes on her; he wanted her to look at him so bad, but she wouldn't—not directly anyway. Setting the precedent that Fred wasn't getting what he wanted was an important step in ending things.

After the incident in the closet, Liv had blocked his number. She'd been on the losing end of life for too long. With things finally at a turning point, she wasn't about to let anyone jerk her around.

The plan was to just act like Fred didn't exist. Whatever had happened between them was water under the bridge in Liv's eyes. Regardless of the threats and sexual blackmail, she was willing to overlook it all if they could just end the whole thing.

She'd considered going to management and telling them about Fred's inappropriate behavior and intimidation. But she decided against it. After all, she'd consensually had an affair with him.

As uncomfortable as the situation had grown, Liv didn't want to create an office fiasco. Maybe they'd decide to let both of them go for engaging in an office fling. She had no way of knowing what the outcome would be.

But the thing she was even more concerned about was angering Fred. She still wanted to keep their secret quiet. Things with Bruce were better than ever, and more than anything, she didn't want to jeopardize that. Some of her strategy was selfish—she was elated to have her family back and refused to lose them again.

But the decision really boiled down to Dustin. Now that he was getting better, she didn't want to create any bumps in the road that might impede his progress. He'd been a part of a broken family long enough.

I'm definitely going to tell Bruce. He deserves that much. I'll beg for his mercy, beg for another chance. But not yet. First, I need to let Dustin heal. I can't do anything that'll risk setting him back.

She saw Fred glaring at her from the corner of her eye.

But what if he tells Bruce before I can?

She took a deep breath and decided that wondering about things that weren't in her control wasn't a game she was willing to play.

Just be cool. That's all you can do.

She could feel his eyes on her, could practically see the steam coming out of his ears.

He'll get over it. It might just take some time.

HAPPINESS OR HELL?

Marta waited patiently, crouched in the darkness.

It was now the third time she'd drugged Dustin. Due to the unique family stress that the Huxleys had constantly dealt with, being tired or sleeping at odd times wasn't anything abnormal. The chaos of the family dynamic was to her benefit.

But today, she wouldn't be using that benefit.

Today, when Bruce returned, she would be pulling the curtain back.

As she studied Dustin's limp body slouched in the chair, she heard the front door open. She remained still, listening to who she knew must be Bruce as he shuffled through the other rooms before finally ascending the stairs. When the door opened, she knew there'd be a certain level of outrage, but she was prepared to keep it under control. She activated the light.

"What the fuck is this?" Bruce cried.

A powerful light was trained on Dustin, still sitting motionless in his chair. Marta crouched over her bowl with strange symbols etched into it, which held the bloated, rotten dove. She kept one hand around the black bird's necrotic neck and the other behind her back.

"Relax," she said. "Everything's fine. Dustin's just—"

Bruce took a quick step toward the boy to check on him, clearly concerned by his motionless state.

Marta whipped the other arm out from behind her back and leveled a silver derringer at his head.

"Don't fucking touch him!"

Bruce raised his hands and stepped backward, looking like he'd just seen a ghost. "Okay, I'm—I'm not moving. But this isn't about Dustin. It's about you and me."

"That's where you're wrong," Marta said.

"Please," he begged.

"It's okay, Bruce. In my estimation, everything is still fixable. But you do have a decision to make—a very *important* decision."

Bruce put his hands together like he was praying. "I'll—I'll do whatever you want . . . Just please, don't hurt him."

"Shut the fuck up for a minute and this'll all make sense. You probably won't believe it, but in just a moment, you won't have a choice."

"What?"

Marta turned her head. "Look at the wall."

Bruce obeyed her command and twisted his head toward Dustin and the light fixed on him.

"Okay, just stay calm."

"What do you see?" she asked.

Bruce focused as best he could, but the only shadows in the light were Marta's and the chair's.

"Your shadow," he replied.

"Now what's missing?"

He furrowed his brow. "I—I don't know."

"Think about what you just said."

She saw the moment of realization hit him like a ton of bricks as it suddenly clicked. He stared at the outline of the chair that his boy was sitting on, but Dustin wasn't represented in its shadow.

"Where . . . where the fuck is Dustin's shadow?" Bruce stammered.

"I gave you your son back . . . Let that sink in. I'll say it again. I gave you your fucking son back!"

"What the hell are you talking about?!" Bruce yelled.

"Actually, come to think of it," Marta continued, ignoring his question, "over the years, I've given a few people their loved ones back. As you can probably imagine, there aren't a lot of people in this world with my skillset. But do you know what the difference between you and all those other people is?"

Bruce shook his head, eyes filled with terror.

With one hand Marta squeezed hard on the flailing, oversized dove as it cried. "They at least had the decency to acknowledge it. To give me what I desired in return. I gave you peace again, and you shit all over me. But thankfully, when I first saw you, I figured you might. I guess I've always had good intuition." She motioned with the gun to the corner of the room. "Go stand over there. Now!"

"All right, just—"

She aimed the gun at his face. "Not a fucking word."

Bruce promptly shuffled into the corner, obeying her commands.

Placing the gun within reach, she picked up a small blade she'd been concealing by her side and cut the necrotic dove open. She decapitated it first, exposing a vile porridge of insects and mushy dead meat. The black and pink tissues pulsated with the perversion that infected it. She then sliced off the broken wings and feet—she'd been forced to mangle the bird out of precaution to pacify it before transport. The bird parts twitched inside the dish. Gutting the bird's belly, she let the remainder of the sickening ooze coat the symbols that littered the bowl.

"What are you . . . You're killing it!" Bruce yelled.

Marta grinned. "I'm not sure if you've noticed, but this bird was long dead before I put my blade in it."

She quickly picked up the gun again and rose, rushing in front of the sloping light. The dish glowed menacingly as she raised it in front of the bulb. The light no longer touched Dustin's motionless body, the shadow created by the putrid bowl and mutilated dove inside it blocking its path.

"You're a fucking loon!" Bruce screamed.

Marta kept the gun on him with her free hand. "Oh, am I? Watch." She gestured to the wall.

Bruce turned, and his eyes instantly bulged. He looked back at the dish, then the wall, several times. A hazy darkness rose from the bowl like smoke from a raging fire, manifesting into a dark shadow on the wall. The wicked particles continued to multiply until a much larger black mass appeared.

He'll see, Marta thought.

As the dove's movement ceased, she pulled the dish down to her side, revealing an impossible sight—the outline of the chair was now occupied. Dustin's shadow had returned. Only now it was much, *much* bigger than it ever was before.

Bruce's bottom lip quivered. "What have you done?"

"I've taken back my charity," she said as a devilish grin overtook her face.

She could see that he was stunned. Bruce's entire world had been turned upside down. Suddenly, everything he ever believed—even the rules of reality as a whole—had shifted.

"What are you talking about?" he asked.

Marta let out a wicked cackle. "There was a darkness inside your boy. One that attaches itself to our shadows, like a parasite. But unlike any tick or leech that can be simply pulled off with any old pair of tweezers, I'm afraid this process is much different. The intricacies of such matters require an attention to detail that few have. One must have arcane knowledge and a mind deeply skilled in the dark arts."

"Why the fuck would you put that thing back inside him?!" Bruce screamed.

"Oh, I'm sorry. Allow me to explain. I didn't put it *back* into him." She wagged her bloody finger. "No, no, no. This is a different . . ." She searched for the words. ". . . *shade* of darkness. And I promise, what lies inside him now is far, *far* worse than anything you've ever seen or even imagined. I certainly wouldn't want to be around him when the sedatives I gave him wear off. No matter how much you pay me . . ."

Tears filled Bruce's eyes. Marta felt indifferent about the agony she knew he must've been feeling. After everything he'd been through, he was finally offered a glimpse at who his son actually was. And just like that, before they could even settle in, he was gone again.

"Marta, please, he's—he's just a child," Bruce begged, tears streaming down his face.

"That is true," Marta said. "But it's already done. When he awakens, he will be a savage the likes of which you've never set eyes on. The type of maniac that's only written about in fiction. Either someone will have to kill him or he will kill them. That much I can promise you."

"You're . . . you're a monster—"

"I am what you made me," she corrected. "But it doesn't have to be this way. I felt the lust and passion inside when we made love. It was more than just fucking. There's something between us. It pains me to have done this to your boy. But our relationship can still be salvaged. As I said before, you have a choice to make. It's a difficult one, but one you'll need to make nonetheless."

Bruce was shaking in the corner like the deepest fears he was never aware of were now rattling his soul. Marta imagined that he had figured the worst thing he had to worry about was covering up his affair. It must be difficult coming to grips with just how wrong he was.

"What choice?" Bruce finally managed.

"All you would need to do is leave this house and not return until later in the evening. Allow Dustin a little . . . one-on-one time with his mother."

"Fuck you!" Bruce yelled.

"Trust me, you're going to want to hear me out."

Bruce pounded the wall. She didn't like seeing him in such a way, but it was necessary.

"As I was saying, give him some time alone with Liv, and once he's finished with her, I'd be willing to extract this new darkness from him before you call the proper authorities after . . . well . . . after whatever he does to her."

Bruce pulled at his hair, clearly tortured by the thought of betraying Liv. "No, I-I won't do it! I can't!"

"I'm offering you a safe life for your son. At his age, he'll be taken to a mental facility—no longer shadowed by the darkness—and probably go on to lead a relatively peaceful existence. And you'll be relieved of your familial burden indefinitely."

Marta moved closer to him, using one bloody finger to lovingly trace over Bruce's face.

"And you'll get to spoil me with nice gifts and fuck me every day for the rest of our lives."

The wrinkle on Bruce's brow sank deeper. "And . . . and what about Liv?"

She smiled. "Well, I'm afraid we can't *all* win."

Bruce put his hand over his face. She watched him pound the wall several more times. He was seeing red, and there was no one to blame but himself.

"Hey!" Marta yelled.

She pulled the trigger of the gun as Bruce looked at her. A flame came out the end of the barrel. It was a lighter— the exact same kind of item that started this entire ordeal.

"I implore you to be smart," Marta said. "Accept my mercy. Otherwise, I'll ruin your marriage. But that really won't matter, though. Because you and Liv will both be dead long before you can get a cup of coffee, let alone a divorce. And that darkness . . . that maniacal, depraved shadow will hang over your son for the rest of his miserable life."

Marta lowered the lighter gun to her side and glared at Bruce. "I guess what I'm saying is, your choice really isn't much of a choice at all, is it?"

THE VISITATION

As Liv peeked into Dustin's room, she felt a bit nervous. It seemed like he was sleeping all the time lately. Considering the extreme metamorphosis he'd gone through, she wasn't ungrateful, more just worried about him. Her instinct had always been to protect her baby, but now that the Dustin she remembered had returned, that urge felt more amplified than ever before.

Rest, sweetie, she thought. *Rest as long as you need.*

Liv carefully closed Dustin's door, then slipped inside her bedroom and changed into her nightgown.

Maybe a little alone time wouldn't be the worst thing in the world. I haven't had a chance to unwind in days.

Part of it was just letting herself relax. Before Marta had left for the night, she'd explained to Liv that Dustin had another perfect day. His progress was almost too incredible to believe.

Liv looked at her phone, and as she checked the time, she furrowed her brow.

Hmm, Bruce should've been home by now . . .

But before she could text him, she heard a pounding on the front door.

Finally. Why doesn't he just come in?

Figuring maybe he had his hands full with groceries, Liv hurried downstairs. But when she opened the door, it wasn't Bruce on the other side.

Fred had a look in his eyes like he'd been drinking. His glassy stare held back rage, and as he pushed his way past Liv, the smell of bourbon was heavy on his breath.

"What the fuck are you doing?!" Liv yelled, closing the door and following him.

Fred didn't say a word. He walked into the living room, then scanned the kitchen and office.

"Where is he?" Fred demanded.

"Who?" Liv asked.

"Don't play stupid with me. I know that asshole's here!" He turned his attention from Liv to the staircase. "Bruce! I'm afraid I've got some bad news!"

"He's not here, dammit!" Liv continued to chase after him, following Fred up the stairs. "You—you can't go up there! My son's asleep!"

Fred checked their bedroom and bathroom carefully before setting his sights on the lone door at the end of the hall.

"I'm not fucking around, Fred!" Liv grabbed hold of his arm. "I'm calling the police!"

"You do that." Fred shook off her grip and took hold of Dustin's doorknob. "But not before I have a little talk with my old friend Bru—"

He opened the door and the wooden hockey stick came swinging out, cracking against the top of Fred's face, creating a massive gash over his hairline. The force of the blow caused the end of the stick to shatter and sent him tumbling backward over the banister.

Liv looked on in horror as Fred landed on the floor neck-first and a sickening crack echoed out. His blood painted the white tile around the entrance upon impact, causing Liv to scream and wail. By the time she returned her attention to her son's open door, Dustin was already charging forward.

"Dustin, no—"

Liv's plea was cut off by the jagged wood in the end of the broken hockey stick entering her abdomen. When she looked into her son's eyes, it wasn't the boy she remembered. His pupils were so dark. Drool leaked from his mouth as he gripped the weapon and thrusted it deeper. The broken stick acted more like a spear, the unforgiving wood at the tip coming to a point like a knife. Blood stained Liv's nightgown as Dustin pinned her against the wall and twisted the bloody handle, rupturing her stomach muscle.

"What are you—?"

Pulling the gory spike out, Dustin stabbed her a second time. This thrust was even stronger and caused her to slam harder against the wall.

"My God, what the fuck are you doing?!" she shrieked.

Liv knew that he'd impaled her when she felt the massive wooden splinter scraping against the wall behind her, generating a vibrating sensation in her torso. The warm red was now saturating her nightgown, and her feet were completely covered in blood as a puddle started to form around her. Mind reeling, she had no idea what to do, but fighting through the shock, Liv realized if she didn't do something, Dustin was going to kill her.

Putting both hands around the hockey stick, Liv used all her might to push herself off the wall. She bulldozed Dustin back against the banister, and he lost his grip and footing. Yanking the fragmented stick from her gut, Liv watched as Dustin got his feet set again, saliva raining from his mouth like a rabid dog.

"I'll eat your meat," Dustin grumbled in a primitive tone. "And you eat mine . . ." He lifted his shirt, slapping his belly.

"Leave me alone!" she cried, deciding to make her move.

She threw the bloody stick at him, hoping to buy a couple seconds, and made a break for the staircase. But as she planted her blood-drenched heel on the wooden step, she slipped. The violent tumble sent her body somersaulting, bones cracking against the steps as her momentum carried her through the railing at the bottom.

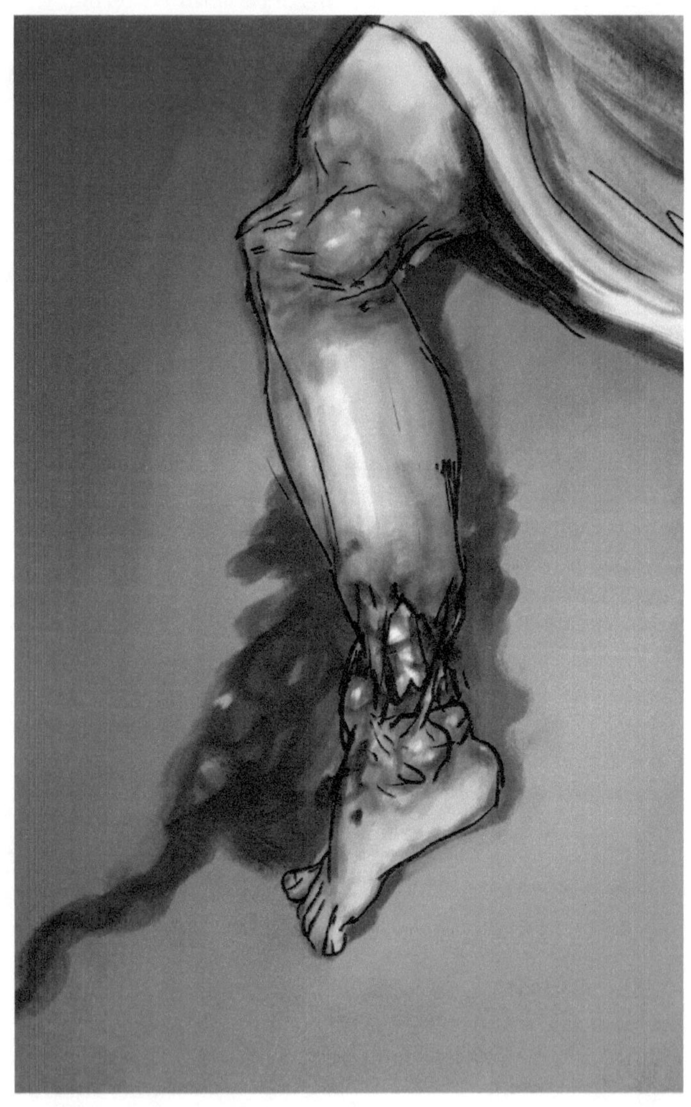

At the foot of the stairs, Liv's kneecap was turned in the complete opposite direction and the ankle on the same leg had a compound fracture. When she saw the bulging backward joint and bone poking out of her crooked foot, she let out a horrified wail.

"*So* hungry," Dustin growled, creeping down the steps with the bloody fragment of the hockey stick still in hand. "So hungry for so, *so* long . . ."

As he approached her, Liv had no idea what to do—the shock was setting in hard.

"You eat me?" Dustin asked.

She didn't understand how Dustin could've transformed into such a monster in a matter of hours. Still stupefied, she couldn't find the words to communicate with him.

Liv cried hysterically as Dustin's fingers curled around her red locks and squeezed tight. Panic exploded through every inch of her body as he dragged her by her hair into the kitchen.

ALL THE GORY DETAILS

Liv looked on helplessly, slumped against the fridge, as Dustin used Fred's belt to tie her arms behind her back. He then returned to Fred and finished stripping him naked. Her son's empty eyes focused on her again.

"Don't move," Dustin growled.

The cleaver propped up on the counter was his weapon of choice. Returning to Fred's body, Dustin straightened out his arm before sizing it up with the blade.

Fred's spine was too mangled for him to resist Dustin's actions. The only defiance he could offer were the whimpers and shock-laced moans he emitted.

As Dustin raised the steel above his head, Fred lost control of his faculties. Piss streamed out of his limp pecker as the edge of the blade connected with his elbow joint. The knife cut through the bone, muscles, and tendons before clanging against the tile floor.

Liv couldn't help letting out a blood-curdling scream. But that didn't stop Dustin from moving in and starting to gnaw on the nub. He'd chosen the piece still attached to Fred's body rather than the limb that had been severed.

With the skin at the end of the wound getting tangled in Dustin's teeth, he bit down. He growled like an animal, shaking his head side to side. A long strip of the rubbery casing ripped up the side of Fred's arm like a massive hang-nail being pulled. Liv watched her boy come away with a mouthful of meat and skin, blood raining down his face as he chewed like a savage during the dawn of man.

The puddle of piss around Fred grew. He let out more sickening moans, but he was so damaged that they were barely audible. As his naked body shook, Dustin took hold of the cleaver again.

Through her screams, she wondered why. Everything had been going so well. Liv could've never predicted such insanity. But figuring out why wasn't going to stop Dustin. Fred's belt was still tight around her wrists, and her ab-dominal wounds were oozing blood. Her leg was mangled beyond repair.

He's going to eat me next! she thought.

As Liv struggled to free herself, the blade came down on Fred's throat. Blood erupted—the partially cut artery was like a spigot. But when the head didn't sever with the initial strike, Dustin rained down several more blows.

Each cut caused the crimson to erupt, reaching far enough to splash Liv's face and pepper dollops of warm blood against her tongue and teeth. But the blood in her mouth didn't stop her wails.

As the cleaver cut deeper, through the spinal bone and neck tissue, Fred's jaw chattered. His eyes rolled up into his skull as the blood cascaded over his detached face.

Dustin lifted Fred's quivering cranium and opened his mouth animalistically. When he bit down on the nose and tore away the chewy cartilage, it was accompanied by a surge of blood and cloudy snot.

Liv's shrieks grew even louder as she watched him pin the head to the floor and worm his teenage fingers behind an eyeball. As Dustin shoved the glistening orb into his mouth, Liv's panic reached the point of no return.

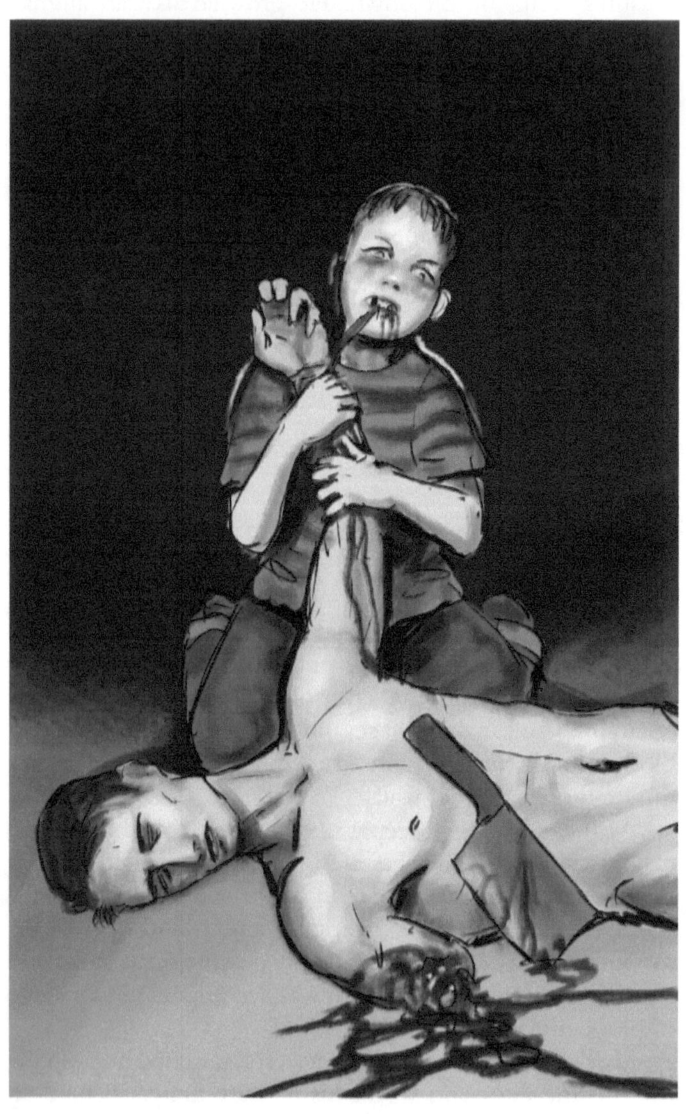

Yanking her arms violently, she knew that she needed to free herself. Liv forced her way through the shock, continuing to try and fight out of the restraint.

A box of cereal and a ceramic jar fell from the top of the fridge, crashing on the floor beside her. As the fragments scraped across the tile, Dustin looked at her.

"Meat!" he yelled.

Liv's screams continued as she looked at the restraint. Pulling manically at the belt, she curved her finger and picked at the buckle. Just as she lifted the prog and felt the leather loosen, a hot flash of burning pain streaked across her forehead.

When her eyes returned to Dustin, she saw his hand around the handle of the cleaver. Liv's vision was soon blurred by the blood that was pouring down from the top of her head. As Dustin knelt in front of her, Liv could feel him grabbing the flapping hunk atop her head. He pulled it back, peeling open the wound before sticking his little, bloody hand inside.

A numbing paralysis overtook Liv, and she felt like her body was short-circuiting. Suddenly, the screaming stopped as the pain flourished inside her head, along with a kneading sensation in her brain. She still wanted to move but couldn't.

When Dustin retrieved his hand from inside her cranium, he was squeezing a soft and mushy clump of brain tissue. She watched on, in a total state of numbness, as he dropped the wet wad into his mouth and chewed before swallowing.

As Dustin licked his fingers clean, he looked back at the gore-caked cleaver on the floor—like his work still wasn't done yet.

CLEANUP CREW

Bruce knew that when he walked through the front door, his life would change forever. There would be images burned into his mind—horrors of an unparalleled nature. Horrors that, whether he chose to accept or not, he was indirectly responsible for. He shouldn't have done it, but he popped an extra pill and a half, knowing that he was definitely going to need it.

Would've just been two of us dead, he reasoned.

But there was that other part of him that he ignored because he wanted to still feel like a good person. That quiet, raspy voice in the back of his head.

Marta is such a better fuck. And with Dustin and Liv out of the way, that's pretty much all we'll be doing. No more stress. No more pain. No more rage. Am I a psychopath? No . . . I felt so good when Dustin was back to normal. I would've done anything to keep all of us together . . . but that wasn't an option.

He shook his head.

This was the only *option she gave you. Get out of your head and get on with it already.*

The door was already unlocked, and as he quietly opened it, Bruce realized nothing could've prepared him for what the kitchen presented.

As he examined the scene from afar, he instantly understood that Marta hadn't been kidding. Had he not chosen to make Liv the sacrificial lamb, there was a good chance that he would've gone down along with her. There was still a chance he might.

The first thing his eyes gravitated to was Liv. Arms tied to the fridge handles, leg mangled, and covered in blood, she couldn't have been more of a mess. Her dumbstruck stare gawked forward, a small section of the top of her head agape with knotty tissue clumped around the open hole.

Jesus fucking Christ.

In front of her was their son. In a massive pool of blood, Dustin hunched over the headless body of a man who was missing part of his arm.

Who . . . who the fuck is that?

After Dustin stretched out one of the man's intestines, he used a knife to cut through it. He squeezed the glistening tube, and the sludge-like partially digested food seeped out. As Dustin shoved the sliced entrail into his mouth and munched, a horrible smell wafted toward Bruce. The smell of rotten eggs and moldy food forced him to put his hand over his mouth.

There might've been tears if the drugs hadn't numbed Bruce to the core. Seeing the hideous husk of the woman he was still convinced that he loved sickened him. But not enough to sway his focus. He crouched down, trying his best not to vomit.

Dustin's rabid actions frightened Bruce, but he had to make a move and wouldn't be offered a better opportunity than the present. After what Dustin had done to Liv and the dead man, Bruce understood the extreme danger of the situation. With his son distracted by the flesh, Bruce figured the element of surprise was the only thing that would allow him a chance to save the boy.

I've gotta go for it . . . It's now or never.

Shooting forward like a spear, Bruce wrapped Dustin up from behind.

As he held him tight, the boy grunted like a wild animal, releasing a barrage of snorts and shrieks. Dusting off his old college wrestling skills, Bruce went for the full nelson but only got half locked in.

Dustin bit down on the top of his father's forearm, and Bruce cried out as the pressure intensified.

"Marta!" Bruce screamed. "What the fuck are you waiting for?!"

"I'm here!" Marta yelled. "I'm here!"

Rushing through the door holding a wooden box, she removed and set the occultic dish on the ground.

"Hurry! H-he's biting through my fucking arm!"

She quickly fished out a rope from the box and tossed it toward Bruce.

"Help me!" he yelled.

"Are you crazy?" Marta looked terrified of the boy. "I'm not touching that savage!"

"I can't tie him up like this . . . I'm gonna have to choke him out first!"

"So do it!"

Bruce quickly muscled his arm out of the half nelson and into a sleeper hold. He and his buddies on his college wrestling team had done it dozens of times. He knew how to cut off the airflow just long enough to put Dustin out, hopefully without hurting him.

As he started to apply pressure, the powerful bite Dustin was applying to Bruce's forearm suddenly loosened. When he stopped fighting, Bruce relinquished his grip on the boy. Holding his arm in agony, he staggered to his feet again. Quickly, he dragged Dustin toward Liv and tied his arms around the refrigerator handles.

Liv let out a hiss of horror that made Bruce jump. When he looked at her destroyed head, the feeling of profound guilt weighed on him. As the death rattle escaped her body, her eyes closed.

"D-d-don't be m-mad at him," Liv somehow managed to say. "I-I'm s-s-sorry, Bruce . . ."

He had no idea what she was talking about, and things were too crazy for him to dwell on it.

God forgive me.

As Dustin's limp body was laid over his now motionless mother's, Marta repositioned the ritual bowl in front of the monstrous shadow. Extracting a white dove from the box, she readied herself. As she cut into the fresh, pure dove's mangled body, just as she had done previously, Bruce watched the smoky particles on the kitchen wall start to dissipate. It didn't take long for the dove's feathers and eyes to transition into the same unnerving colors. The hideous cries of the animal carried on.

The newly blackened dove with red eyes struck terror into Bruce. He watched as Marta quickly shoved the malignant bird into the wooden box. But the creature fought back, pecking her hand in a rage before she could fasten the lock, causing her to cry out.

"Ouch! You stupid creature!"

Marta lifted the box, trying to ensnare the dark dove again, but the oversized bird wailed and emitted a demonic shriek before fluttering out the front door.

"Dammit!" Marta yelled.

"Forget about the fucking bird!" Bruce yelled. "We've got bigger problems!"

"No, not *we*." Marta turned back from the open door and looked at Bruce. "We agreed on this already. My part is done. The rest of this is up to you."

"But . . . I-I don't know if I can do this alone," Bruce said, tears starting to streak down his face.

"You must be strong, my darling. You're so close."

She quickly approached him, sticking her tongue in his mouth as she kissed him passionately. While Bruce wanted anything but a kiss at that moment, he knew it wouldn't be wise to challenge her. He would need to get through chaos before he could figure out what his next steps were.

"One moment of horror for a lifetime of bliss," Marta whispered. "Contact me once it is finished."

"I will," Bruce said.

She looked back at Liv and Dustin, both motionless and tied to the fridge, then back to Bruce.

"Forget about them," Marta said. "In just a short time, this will all seem like a bad dream. I love you, Bruce."

Bruce bit his lip. "I . . ."

He looked at Liv's mangled corpse, ashamed to say it in front of her. But it was his new life. It was what he'd chosen.

"I love you too."

When Marta left, Bruce pulled the phone from his pocket and dialed the police. Before he pressed the call button, he looked down at Dustin.

"I'm sorry, Son . . ." Bruce whispered. "This is the best I can offer you."

THE STATION

Marta sat in the car, patiently waiting. It had started to rain a short time ago, and the occasional flare of lightning kept her entertained. That and the thought of the new life she was beginning. She had a sexy man by her side and more financial security than she could ever dream of.

You finally found the right one, she thought.

The situation from the evening prior seemed clear-cut enough. Dustin had finally snapped, and the trail of violence he'd left behind played in their favor. His countless drawings of macabre and murderous imagery painted him in a terrible light. This included the illustration Marta was happy to hand over in which Dustin all but confessed to Spud's murder. It was the ace up her sleeve that she'd been waiting for the perfect moment to lay down. It also didn't hurt that Dustin had taken a decent-sized hunk out of Bruce's forearm, further proving what was already obvious.

It all lines up. History of mental illness leads to a bloodbath for the ages. If they need further confirmation, I can always add my two cents. I'm sure they'll want to interview me at some point too. I'll really lay it on thick.

When the car door opened, Marta jumped. She watched Bruce plop down in the passenger seat.

Bruce stared forward blankly. The bandaging around his forearm and dried blood on his clothing made him look like an escaped lunatic.

"How did it go?" Marta asked.

He didn't respond, instead opting to stare at the storm.

Marta placed her hand on the side of his face gently and pulled it toward her. "The hard part's over now. You can forget what came before and finally live your life the way it was meant to be lived. With freedom. With excitement." Her hand slid down to his crotch and squeezed his prick. "With satisfaction."

"Please, not right now," Bruce whispered.

She wasn't offended by his request. She loved him—or at least what he represented for her—and understood that he was hurt. She wanted to comfort him. To help rebuild his confidence.

"I know you'll get past it," Marta said. "You wouldn't have made it this far otherwise. But . . . I do need you to tell me what happened. Because of my own involvement, there is a certain amount of detail I require, merely for my own peace of mind."

Bruce continued to vacantly stare forward. "As horrible as it was, it couldn't have worked out any better for us."

"How so?" Marta asked.

"They identified the dead man in my house. He was a coworker of Liv's that she was having an affair with."

Marta tried her best not to smirk.

"Apparently, the police examined each of their phones and found text messages between them . . . I guess that's why he was there." He turned to her. "They actually felt bad for me . . ."

Marta allowed herself to smile. "That's wonderful."

Bruce turned back to the storm. "They said they're going to forensically examine the contents of Dustin's stomach, along with the rest of the weapons used in the murders. I can't imagine they'll find anything that suggests your involvement. In short, you . . . don't have anything to worry about."

As Marta watched him, Bruce's gaze remained fixed on the dark clouds. She imagined he might be looking at the aerial chaos as a metaphor for his life, or at least his past.

"That's all I needed to know," Marta said.

Bruce let his fingers coast over the bandaged bite wound on his arm. "Can you promise me something?"

Marta's heart fluttered with intrigue. "Perhaps . . . I suppose that depends on what you want me to promise."

"Just as soon as this mess is sorted . . . promise me we'll start looking for another house. I-I can't go back there." Tears beaded down his cheeks. "I can't stay in that house."

She grabbed hold of his trembling hand and stroked it gently. "Of course, sweetie."

Bruce bit his lip a moment, trying to hold it together. "I love you."

She smiled at him, wide as the day they'd first met. "I love you too."

YEARS
LATER

THE GOOD LIFE

Bruce loved looking out through the cabin's glass walls. He sipped his wine and let it rest on his tongue. The lakeview was idyllic. Being surrounded by nature and separated from humanity helped him a great deal. Every day was calmer than the last. Sometimes, they wouldn't see anyone for months, and he preferred it that way.

His eyes shifted from the wonderous décor to the laptop screen. The website Huxley's Antiquities displayed. Bruce shook his head.

Finally time to unload this thing, he thought.

Bruce stared at the initials *B.H.* etched into the side of the lighter. The military general's Zippo was now officially an antique. He was glad that was the case. Hanging on to the gift only brought up thoughts of darkness and discomfort. Bruce would've preferred to be rid of it some time ago, but he wasn't about to sell it before it became antique age and lose out on the profit.

Marta had just finished paying for an online ad campaign for the lighter. These days, she was more social than he was. Bruce liked to take care of most of his business online. And as he looked at the number of views on the Zippo's listing, he was pleased to see that it appeared he'd be sending it off soon.

Over a quarter million views already!

Unlike Bruce, Marta occasionally enjoyed going into town to schmooze with the locals. Since he'd used his management experience from Carnegie's to launch his own collectibles business, Marta had helped him make the store successful. Lately, Marta had been buying items in bulk from local vendors and estate sales. They had some spaces they rented in town so they could store inventory until they could fence it and turn a profit.

Not that they truly needed to do much to generate income. Bruce was already well off, and Marta had sold the remaining black dove for a handsome fee some time ago. Their existing balances were all they'd probably ever need.

Bruce spread some fig jam onto a cracker and shoved it in his mouth. He chewed, savoring the flavor, before washing it down with another sip of his wine.

As he brought the glass back down, from the corner of his eye, he caught a glimpse of it: the discolored patch of flesh from the bitemark on his forearm—what would be the last remaining memory of his darkest deed once he unloaded the Zippo lighter.

He felt his breast pocket. While he rarely used the lighter anymore, he still carried it with him every day—just like the scars Dustin had left upon him. He wasn't sure if it was guilt, but in a strange way, it comforted him. Letting go of it was going to be a real test, but it was the only way he'd truly be able to move on.

While his days were mostly just leisurely stretches of relaxation, once in a while Bruce still had trouble during the evenings. Despite having separated himself from anything to do with his life before Marta, the many ghastly images from years past still haunted him.

Liv's head pulled apart.

Dustin's bloody mouth and hateful eyes.

The dead look and pure horror on Liv's face.

The final gawk of utter confusion when Dustin was led off to the mental institution.

If there's a Hell, I'm g—

Bruce's phone pinged, interrupting his thought.

The text message was from Marta.

The items are bigger than I thought, she wrote. *I had to get a rental truck to haul them all. But I'm gonna need help loading and unloading them. Can you come and meet me on Edgecrest Road, near the old diner?*

Bruce scrunched his face in annoyance.

Jesus fucking Christ . . . what'd she go and buy now?

He was tired of ripping his nut lifting her old junk all the time. With the experience he had in the business, Bruce knew how to be calculated about what he bought. While she had some good finds, Marta wasn't quite there yet. Bruce was always happy to try and make a little extra money, but if he was going to be lugging random junk around, he wanted to be sure it sold.

He shook his head before typing back.

Give me a few.

THE MEETING

The fuck is she all the way out at Edgecrest for? Bruce wondered. *There's nothing out here. What a dumb place to meet.*

He was getting tired of the smelly local antique dealers. While he appreciated Marta's enthusiasm to get so involved in the business, it was almost a little too much sometimes. This wasn't the first time he'd had to drive many miles to somewhere inconvenient.

As the old diner came into view, he could see the plain white rental truck parked alongside Marta's SUV. As he pulled into the parking lot, he noticed the ugliness of the dilapidated building.

This looks more like a spot for a drug deal. Where is she?

Bruce hopped out of his car and felt the hot sun beating down on him. The entire road was quiet, all but for his footsteps. As he made his way around the box truck, a man stepped out from behind it.

"Hi there," the man said, tipping his hat. "You must be Bruce, I'm guessing?"

Bruce studied the dark-haired young man. His hat, sunglasses, and mustache made him look like he was on a stakeout. He was a bit taller than him, but not by much.

"Yeah." Bruce held his hand out. "And you are?"

"Mark Clay, owner of Clay's Collectibles." He shook his hand. "It's a pleasure to meet you."

"Same."

"Your wife bought quite a few pieces."

Bruce huffed. "Yeah, she goes a little nuts sometimes." He was already bored with the conversation. He just wanted to get the haul done and go home. Glancing around the area, Bruce furrowed his brow. "Where is she?"

"Oh!" Mark pointed to the back of the old diner. "I guess she really had to piss. Said she'd be right back. I'll tell you, though, she drives a hard bargain, but just has a knack for getting what she wants. But you're her husband—I'm sure you know that already." He chuckled.

Something about the way the man talked made Bruce uneasy. While it was possible Marta had to relieve herself, something just didn't seem right.

The man looked down at Bruce's arm. "Holy smokes, that's one nasty-ass scar. I've got a few myself, but yeesh. How'd you get it?"

Bruce didn't like the personal questions but decided to appease him. "Just a dog bite from a while back."

"Shit, he got you good," Mark said. "Was it your dog?"

"Yeah."

"If he got me that good, I'da put 'em down. Did you have to put him down after that, Bruce?"

A strange sensation bubbled inside Bruce, causing him to hesitate. He didn't want to answer, but Mark was annoyingly persistent. "Yeah."

"That's a shame . . . I can't blame you, I suppose. What kinda dog was it? Because looking at the size of that bite, it's very concentrated. Most dogs got bigger jaws. Yeah, if I was just guessin', I'd say that bite looks more like it came from a human."

Bruce's heartrate exploded—the feeling in his gut was of pure dread. "Well, good thing no one's fucking asking you." He turned his head toward the back of the diner. "Marta! Where the hell are you?"

The man stretched, slipping his hand behind his back. "Plus, if Spud was already dead, how could he have bitten you? Doesn't make a whole lotta sense."

Bruce's jaw dropped. As his head snapped back toward the man, he realized that he wasn't who he'd said he was. It was such a subtle thing that he'd easily missed, but the sun beating down only made it crystal clear: While the man before him stood just the same as Bruce, there was one very odd trait that inflated Bruce's abdomen with dread.

He didn't cast a shadow.

By the time Bruce realized the anomaly, it was already too late. The stun gun connected with Bruce's neck, causing his body to go limp. And just as he dropped to the ground, a big boot came down on his face.

AMONG THE TREES

Dustin set the sunglasses on the passenger seat of the rental truck. It was getting dark now, and they were no longer necessary. He also removed the hat and wig, as it was making his scalp itchy. Turning down the dark road, he saw the familiar path.

He carefully maneuvered the truck between the trees. Trying his best not to hit anything, he really took his time. Dustin had already spent a great deal of it on research. Luckily, finding a place with such complete isolation close to his father wasn't actually too difficult, considering where Bruce and Marta had chosen to settle down.

The wooded area he was on wasn't even a road, just a section of forest with trees that were far enough apart from each other to allow him access. When the headlights reflected against the windshield of his car he'd stashed in the woods, he knew he was finally where he needed to be. He parked the truck and twisted off the ignition.

When he opened the gate of the truck, the inside of the box didn't get much brighter. Dusk was upon them. Dustin unwrapped Bruce from the blanket that covered him, revealing binding around all his limbs, earplugs, and a dirty rag in his mouth. His moans and pleas were muffled.

"Long time no see," Dustin said, removing the earplugs and gag from Bruce's head and tossing them deeper into the truck.

"W-what the fuck is this?" Bruce screamed. "You're—you're supposed to be institutionalized!"

"I came all this way . . . dyed my mustache for you, and that's the first thing you've got to say?"

"Where the fuck is Marta?!"

"Oh, she's here. Or at least she was for a while," Dustin said, pointing to the back of the truck.

Leaning against the wall sat Marta's motionless body. She had a plastic bag over her head, but it was transparent enough to see the unmistakable look of death in her eyes and the paleness of her normally warm complexion.

"Did you think I was gonna separate you guys? How could I? Clearly, she was more important to you than anyone else . . ."

"You sick fuck! What did you—?"

Dustin grabbed the rag and shoved it back into his mouth.

"I think you've done enough talking. It's time for you to listen." He removed a cigarette from his inside pocket and promptly lit it. "Aw, c'mon, don't look at me like that. I know it's a nasty habit. But extreme trauma can make you do things that're a helluva lot worse than smoking, right?"

He turned around and looked out into the woods.

"I know what you're thinking: How? I wouldn't be the first juvenile to get sprung. Truth is, most kids who kill people at the age I was get reintroduced back into society. Not that *I* killed anyone—you damn well know that."

Dustin flicked the ash on his smoke.

"You see, I might not have been awake when you and that witch were plotting, but that thing . . ." He struggled with his emotions. "That fucking thing you put inside me was. And when something's inside of you, driving . . . you learn a lot."

He took another massive drag from the cigarette before snubbing it out and putting the butt in his pocket. Dustin didn't plan on leaving any evidence behind—he couldn't afford to get in trouble again.

"That's not really the special part of all this, though." He considered if he should even tell Bruce. "Well, I suppose it's worth saying only because it is pretty goddamn remarkable."

While pulling out another smoke from his inside pocket, Dustin leaned against the truck as close to Bruce as he could get. He exhaled the big puff of smoke in his face.

"I was ready to let it all go. It wasn't easy spending so many years around a bunch of lunatics and people who thought I was crazy when I wasn't. After all that, when I found out I was leaving, I just wanted to forget. When I got out, I got a job. Went to some group meetings—that's where I got stuck on these things . . . again."

When he held up the cigarette, Bruce furrowed his brow as if to say *Again?*

"Smoking helped me relax. You remember, right, Bruce? Just like back in college."

Dustin watched as Bruce's eyes widened and confusion completely overtook him.

Shaking his head, Dustin laughed. "Can't believe you almost didn't date me because of these. You would've been doing me a favor!"

Dustin could feel the rage inside starting to swell.

"Because God knows you need a fucking cigarette when you're trapped in your son's body!"

***

The spit flew off Dustin's lips as he wore a mask of his mother's fury. Liv's hatred continued to spew.

"That's right," Liv growled. "I guess that witch"—Dustin pointed to Marta's corpse—"must've fucked up, because the wires got crossed! And now, who knows if our son will ever get to live his own goddamn life!"

His eyes glossed over, and a tear dripped down the side of Bruce's face. He was starting to shake uncontrollably. Through his gag, he begged, but Liv couldn't make out what he was saying.

"He's still here with me," Liv said. "I can still tap into Dustin's feelings, memories, and trauma . . . But it's like he's just in the background. Everything he does is up to me now."

Liv considered what she'd just said, almost feeling bad about what she was thinking.

"But when I—I mean *we*—when we got out of that place and saw your little ad … I knew one thing for sure. Whether it had to be by Dustin's hand or not, I wasn't gonna let you and that slut get away with this."

Taking another puff of the smoke, Liv motioned Dustin's body to French inhale, looking out into the woods and then up at the clouds.

"Sometimes, it's just fate." Dustin stared at the cigarette. "Even though I know these things aren't good for us, I needed something. But I ran into a little annoyance. I kept losing my lighters or buying more than I needed. I decided that I would get something nice. Maybe if I had a decent, respectable light, I could build some kind of discipline."

Dustin took another drag.

"So I got to thinking about nice lighters, and I remembered when I gave someone a *really* nice lighter once—a collectible, in fact. But to do a search and have that beautiful antique pop up right before our eyes . . . now what are the odds?"

Dustin walked closer to Bruce.

"I bet you thought you didn't have to worry. I bet after you pulled that demon out of my son and left him holding the bag, you thought you were safe. But you were wrong." Dustin pointed at Marta again. "And the truth is, I could do the same to you as I did to her. But that's . . . that's not why we're here."

He exhaled another mass of smoke out of his nose.

"I want you to stay here alone. Become one with the darkness—the same way you forced my son to. I want you to think about every fucking thing you've been hiding all these years."

Dustin nodded, glaring at the back of the truck.

"And maybe, if you get hungry enough, you can crawl your way over to Marta and see if she can provide you with some nourishment. Because I want you to stay alive long enough to really think about what Hell's gonna feel like when your sorry ass is burning in it."

After removing the gag from Bruce's mouth, Dustin also cut his hands free.

"Liv, wait!" Bruce begged. "You don't understand, I—I didn't have a choice!"

Before he could reach the truck's rear, Dustin grabbed hold of the gate strap. "And that's where we disagree. There's always a choice. And this is mine."

He jumped off the bumper, pulled down the backend, and quickly slapped a lock on it. As the screams and pounding commenced, Dustin put his cigarette out and slipped the butt in his pocket again. Walking over toward the other parked vehicle, he took a deep breath.

Yell all you like, Liv thought. *It won't make a difference.*

As Dustin opened the car door, Liv's urges forced him to light yet another cigarette. She needed all the stress relief possible, so the smoke seemed imperative.

As the car started up, Dustin looked at the picture on the dashboard. It was the same one Liv had kept on her desk for so many years: the three of them smiling outside of the water park, enjoying the lovely afternoon.

Dustin took a few big puffs of the cigarette until the ember was piping hot, then Liv forced him to use the tip to slowly burn Bruce's face out of the picture.

DAYS
LATER

IN THE DARK

The inside of the truck smelled like piss and shit. The air was thick enough to chew. Bruce was so weak and malnourished that he hadn't moved in hours. It was so dark inside the truck that he could hardly see anything. He continued to stare into the darkness while thinking about what Liv had said before locking him inside.

Hell is at arm's length now, he thought. *I couldn't really eat her . . . could I?*

After running through it inside his head countless times, he concluded that there was only one choice. If he didn't, he was going to die—he probably wouldn't make it through the night. In spending so much time alone in the dark, he'd become intimately attuned to his body, and as a result, he knew the life was leaking out of it. He could feel it. And there was a strong likelihood that if he didn't make his move now, he might not even have the strength to eat at a later time.

Fuck, this is sick! How could he—I mean she—*do this to me?! God-fucking-dammit!*

He knew crying about it in his head wasn't going to do anything but let more precious time tick by. The only thing he could really see in the pitch black was the outline of the white plastic bag over Marta's head.

Maybe I'll just eat some of her legs . . .

As he crawled toward her, doing his best to conserve his energy, he couldn't believe he was actually going to do it. The already overwhelming smell of ammonia and stale feces that dominated the box truck only intensified as he got closer to Marta.

She must've relieved herself before she died.

Feeling his hand mash into the feces on the floor, Bruce was too exhausted to outwardly react with disgust. He didn't even have enough energy to shake it off; he just let the clumps of pasty shit remain caked on his hand.

Who knows where Dustin parked this truck . . . If I can just stay alive for a few more days, maybe someone can still find me.

He thought about how he'd pounded and screamed for many days. How he'd exerted so much energy trying to attract someone's—anyone's—attention.

It's my only chance.

As he lifted Marta's leg, he noticed something strange—it was still warm.

My God . . . sh-she's still alive!

Feeling a faint pulse in her ankle, Bruce remained in total shock. He was too weak to muster energy to speak. His mind started racing again.

"It's okay . . ." Marta whispered, clearly trying to find the strength. "Eat me."

Bruce's eyes started to tear up. He could now see that the bag hung loosely on her head, still distant enough to allow her faint breathing. At one point, he'd wondered why her body hadn't started to stink, and now he had his answer. He'd just assumed the smell of the piss and shit had overpowered any other scent inside the box truck.

As a violent shudder overtook Bruce, he considered it. Eating a dead person was bad enough, but eating someone who was alive was even sicker.

But what choice do I have?

"Just . . . eat some," she said. "Get strength . . ."

Despite his stomach bucking at the nauseating thought, Bruce still brought the leg up to his mouth.

You've got to go all the way, Bruce thought. *This is your last chance. Get it while it's fresh.*

As he positioned the back of her calf and unhinged his jaw, some of the pasty feces spread across her skin. But it was so dark he only realized when he was already tasting it. Biting down on the clump of meat as hard as could, Bruce was eventually able to rip a chunk away. Using the warm blood as lubrication allowed him to get it down quicker, swallowing the throbbing wad along with the grainy shit.

My God . . . this is Hell!

But as he slumped onto the floor and sensed the meat falling to his belly, Bruce felt the instant shot of vigor that the mouthful had provided him.

"Keep going," Marta begged.

Bruce knew if he was smart, he would listen to her. Especially while she wanted him to continue.

"Doesn't it hurt?" he finally managed to say.

There was no answer.

Straightening up and taking hold of the bleeding leg, he realized that she was probably on the verge of death. Marta was most likely numb, and the fact that she wanted to offer herself as a sacrifice was almost fitting.

Fucking cunt—she got me into this whole mess.

As he dove in for another bite, Bruce was grateful that he couldn't see her wound—it helped make feeding on her easier than it should've been. Feeling around with his tongue and mouth, he located the bleeding flesh and worked toward the edge of the rip like he was attacking an extra-chewy apple that had already been bitten.

Marta kept quiet as he continued to tear clump after clump of meat off her leg, until the backside of the limb was like an ear of buttery corn that had been stripped of all the kernels. Feeling he'd gotten his fill, he set her bloody leg on the ground and crawled away.

Bruce decided that staying close to her after he'd just eaten the majority of her leg felt weird. And he wanted to get away from the smell of bodily waste so he didn't vomit up the meat.

As he felt around in the darkness, he used his sense of smell to find the sweet spot between where Marta had relieved herself and the corner of the truck that he'd been using as the bathroom. It would've been so much easier if there was any kind of light.

Light—that's what started this entire fucking thing in the first place, Bruce thought, recalling what Liv had said about finding the general's lighter after an internet search. *What are the odds? If only Marta hadn't put up that fucking ad for the . . .*

Suddenly it hit him.

The lighter!

Bruce frantically reached for his pocket, wondering how he could've forgotten about it.

Maybe I can burn my way out of this fucking box!

It sounded dangerous, but anything was worth a try at this point. He was just glad to have another option. As he retrieved the lighter, he didn't wait to use it. But when the light came on, he was faced with a new revelation.

On the ground in front of him sat a familiar bowl with strange symbols. It was filled with blood, various bird parts, and black feathers. Next to the dish was the gag that Dustin had removed from his mouth, along with the earplugs.

"Fuck . . ."

The hair stood up on Bruce's neck as he felt a presence beside him. When he turned, he saw Marta, still with the bag over her head, kneeling beside him in a pool of blood. A monstrous shadow projected against the wall behind her, towering over them.

"My turn!" Marta screamed, pouncing on him.

When the light cut out, he screamed.

It wasn't as bad as it could've been. As Marta's teeth and fingernails tore into Bruce and he felt the agony of his flesh being ripped apart, he was grateful that at least he didn't have to watch.

FULL CIRCLE

With darkness surrounding the car, Liv finished watching the short documentary and had to wonder if she'd gone too far. The video was produced by a channel called All the Gory Details and discussed the Cumberland Caveman Killer.

Such a strange pseudonym was hard to forget. Liv recalled an advertisement on the TV back at Fred's house years ago about the exact same sicko. Apparently, the case had seen a resurgence in popularity online.

Small world, Liv thought.

Being the pilot of Dustin's body also gave Liv access to all of her son's memories. After learning Dustin had been possessed by multiple entities—the worst being the one that had slaughtered her body—she knew there was only one way that Bruce deserved to die.

He needed to know what it was like, Liv thought. *He needed to know and now he does.*

The Cumberland Caveman Killer had earned his name by living like a savage off the land of an old, abandoned monastery. The maniac had bludgeoned various hikers and backpackers to death with rocks and other primitive tools created from things he'd found in the forest. He ate most all of his victims, but not before offering up some of his own body to them.

The disturbed murderer was killed by one of his victims who had been taken captive and forced to eat several pieces of the Caveman's thigh. Only then was the full extent of his crimes discovered: A cave that housed the bones of nearly a dozen bodies. A cave that many children in the area considered to be haunted and would visit on dares.

The cave that poor Kelsey Emit ended up inside . . .

Going off of what Dustin's memory recalled about the demon's history was horrifying enough, but after finishing the video with all the gory details, she wondered if it was selfish to unleash that thing back into the world.

What do I know? Who even knows if that thing could be destroyed? Better that it be in the middle of nowhere, confined, than anywhere else.

Torturing Marta to get an understanding of how to go about transferring these entities hadn't been hard. She gave up the info with relative ease. She'd explained where her books and supplies were. But as smart as Marta was, she couldn't seem to figure out why Liv—or Dustin, as she saw it—would want to procure such information.

We'll see if she likes not being in control for the rest of her miserable goddamned life.

Liv chuckled, looking into the rearview mirror at the black birdcage in the backseat. What Marta and everyone outside of Dustin and Liv didn't realize was that lost evil is never truly lost—it's just waiting.

And in their case, drawn to its last affair.

She recalled all the days trapped in Dustin's body that she'd spent locked inside the mental institution. Her efforts were relentless as she tried to use her adult rationality to convince those in charge that Dustin was better. That the murders were all a big mistake and such thoughts hadn't and wouldn't ever manifest in the way they had on that one horrible night.

But more specifically, Liv recalled the window she had looked out of every day in the recreation area of the nuthouse. And while she didn't dare mention it to any of the caretakers, she saw it: the black, malignant dove in all its disgusting glory, perched on a tree branch, just waiting.

Waiting for the day Dustin got out.

This was fate, Liv thought. *How could it not be? The bird, the lighter . . . and now, this feeling . . .*

Ever since she'd left Bruce behind several days ago, she'd gotten the feeling. It was like Dustin was communicating to her through feelings. Urging his mother onward.

I still don't get it, though . . . Why would Dustin want us to come back here?

As she slipped the phone into Dustin's pocket, she could only distract herself for so long. The once beautiful house that Liv's mother was so excited to have purchased was no longer so pretty. The overgrown weeds, busted shingles, and broken windows made it look like a crack house.

This is where it all started.

She wasn't surprised that no one wanted to buy the property. After the horrible things that had happened there, maybe Bruce was right—Alice was an anomaly. No one else wanted to live in a house of death. It was too much for most people. Still, she couldn't figure out why it wasn't too much for Dustin—why his consciousness loomed in the background begging her to bring him full circle. Especially considering his memories of that horrible bald-headed woman.

The Mother of Bliss . . . Liv thought, a shudder running down her spine.

It felt like Dustin was urging Liv out of the car.

She piloted her son's body through the night, past the NO TRESPASSING sign, and around the back of the house. Next to some spray-painted obscenities that had been left around the rear of the structure, she saw the back door was open.

The basement . . . It was almost like she could hear Dustin whispering in her ear.

As Liv made her way inside, she felt her heart pounding. But she pushed herself forward and opened the basement door, not knowing how long she would have the courage to act. With each tired groan of the old wooden stairs, she finally made it to the bottom.

The many faces of the disturbed followers and The Mother of Bliss were nowhere to be found. Just darkness. Without their fearless leader, the warped members of The Transcenders had been vanquished and instead replaced by the kind, ghostly complexion of an older-looking woman.

"Liv . . . sweetie," Alice whispered. "It's so good to see you again . . . I've missed you."

"Mom?" Liv whispered.

As the words came out of her mouth, her emotion made Dustin's lips quiver.

"It's okay, sweetie," Alice said. "I know you're scared, but it's time for you to let go. You've done what you needed to. You've found justice. Dustin's all grown up now, and it's only right that he gets to live his life. Okay?"

The tears poured out of Dustin's eyes—Liv knew her mother was right. She'd been so focused on revenge that she'd been blinded and inadvertently put her son's needs on the back burner. Dustin must've sensed it and known this was the only way—that's why he'd brought them back here. She wanted more than anything to give Dustin his free will back. To allow him to live the life he'd never gotten to.

"I—I know, Mom," Liv said. "I just needed you to say it. But I understand now."

Alice extended her spectral arm toward Dustin, as if to help pull her daughter out of him.

Moments later, Liv's pale entity drained out of Dustin and poured into the darkness alongside her mother.

***

Dustin stood, mystified, staring with glossy eyes at the two women who'd been most important in his life. The two women who'd meant *everything* to him.

"It's okay, honey," Liv said. "I'm with Grandma now. It's time for you to go."

"But . . . I-I don't wanna leave you," Dustin cried.

"We'll never truly leave you, Dustin," Liv said.

"It's true," Alice added.

"We'll always be looking down on you," Liv whispered. "You've got a life to live. And it's *long* overdue."

"Don't you worry about us," Alice said. "We've got each other. Everything's going to be just fine. Okay?"

"O-o-okay," he whispered.

"Go on, then," Alice said with a smile. "I love you, Dustin, but this house is abandoned with good reason, and you don't need to spend any more time in here than necessary."

"Love you too, Grandma . . ."

"I love you, Son," Liv said.

Dustin wiped his tears. "I . . . I love you too, Mom."

As he made his way up the stairs, he tried to keep his emotions bottled, but he quickly unraveled once he reached the top. The idea that he'd just seen his mother and grandmother for the last time was heavy.

But on the other hand, finally getting a chance to live his life, now that everyone else was through living it for him, felt like the greatest gift he'd ever been bestowed with.

He was kind of grateful that his mother had exacted revenge. What his father had done was beyond wrong—it was evil. In the process of preparing for the confrontation, Liv had taken many steps to help him stabilize his life.

She'd set up an apartment for him and got him a decent job that he was looking forward to returning to. Just doing anything normal—anything himself—would be something special. Setting up such things would've been a monumental task for him to undertake on his own, but now, he could actually focus on healing and figuring out what his life was supposed to be about.

That's it, Dustin thought. *No more tears.* He wiped his face. *That's not what Mom wants. She wants me to live. She wants me to—*

A loud popping sound echoed through the room, interrupting his thoughts. The strange noise sounded very much like knuckles cracking. As Dustin turned away from the basement steps and looked across the kitchen toward the exit, he saw a tall shadow.

The man was featureless aside from his lengthy hair and oddly long fingers. As Dustin watched the eerie outline, he remained frozen in place, a sense of panic overtaking him. He wanted to scream, but his jaw held stiff. Dustin was relegated to the role of spectator, watching the thing.

It didn't say a word.

It just cracked its knuckles again and took a step closer.

ABOUT THE AUTHOR

Aron Beauregard is no longer actually Aron Beauregard. He's a guy with the spirit of a local roofer who tragically fell to his doom during a trivial Riverdance accident. He has formally retired from writing books and can now be seen dancing at all times while speaking with a phony Irish accent. When he's not dancing, he's fielding calls on new potential projects—not book projects, but like replacing people's old roof shingles and whatnot. He wants word to get out and people to know that sometimes getting possessed isn't scary or horrifying—like the tale you've just finished reading. Sometimes it's just weird and cringe . . . And instead of doing the really cool stuff that you actually enjoy doing, you're forced to do stupid, outdated dances.

FILM & TV RIGHTS

Homewreckers was written with both the big and small screen in mind. For inquiries on obtaining film or television rights, please email:
AronBeauregardHorror@gmail.com

SERIOUS INQUIRIES ONLY.

FOR SIGNED BOOKS, MERCH, AND
EXCLUSIVE ITEMS VISIT:

ABHORROR.COM

AB HORROR FUN FACT

After going super viral in July of 2023, Aron Beauregard's "Playground" books have sold countless copies and ruffled serious feathers. The incendiary series has triggered the masses in such a way that the author still receives the occasional death threat. If you'd like to know what all the fuss and outrage is about, check out "Playground" and "Playground: Child of Divorce." If you'd like to submit a death threat, those are also very much appreciated as the author has been living based on spite alone for some time.

HORROR WITHOUT BOUNDARIES

AB HORROR CHALLENGE

To participate in the AB Horror Challenge, simply read or listen to any Aron Beauregard book, then take to social media and share your reaction. Talk about how you felt surviving the nastiest or the most emotional parts in your videos or posts, and then tag the author for a chance at free signed books and more! To increase your chances, TikTok videos are highly encouraged! Tag the author: @ABHorror